P9-CDL-204

ALSO BY ROBERT OLMSTEAD

River Dogs

Soft Water

A Trail of Heart's Blood Wherever We Go

America by Land

Stay Here with Me

Coal Black Horse

FAR BRIGHT STAR

A NOVEL BY

ROBERT OLMSTEAD

ALGONQUIN BOOKS OF CHAPEL HILL

2009

Published by

ALGONQUIN BOOKS OF CHAPEL HILL
Post Office Box 2225
Chapel Hill, North Carolina 27515-2225

a division of
WORKMAN PUBLISHING
225 Varick Street
New York, New York 10014

This is a work of fiction. While, as in all fiction, the literary
perceptions and insights are based on experience, all names, characters,
places, and incidents either are products of the author's imagination or
are used fictitiously.

Library of Congress Cataloging-in-Publication Data
Olmstead, Robert.
Far bright star / by Robert Olmstead.—1st ed.
p. cm.
ISBN-13: 978-1-56512-592-6
1. Soldiers—United States—Fiction.   2. Villa, Pancho, 1878–1923—
Fiction.   3. United States. Army—History—Punitive Expedition
into Mexico, 1916—Fiction.   4. Mexican-American Border Region—
Fiction.   5. Revolutionaries—Mexico—Fiction.   I. Title.
PS3565.L67F37 2009
813'.54—dc22   2008041858

10 9 8 7 6 5 4 3 2 1
First Edition

Think when we talk of horses, that you see them
Printing their proud hoofs i' the receiving earth . . .

—WILLIAM SHAKESPEARE, *Henry V*

FAR BRIGHT STAR

1

THUS FAR THE SUMMER of 1916 had been a siege of wrathy wind and heated air. Dust and light. Sand and light. Wind and light.

There was drought and the land was parched and dry and the country bleached, burned out, and furnacelike. At first, dogs attended the troopers, but then they experienced a plague of fleas, so the order went out to shoot the dogs.

It was 125 miles south of the international line in Colonia Dublán where the expedition had established its headquarters. They were well supplied. They shipped in tons of material by rail, truck, and mule team and employed thousands of civilian workers. The cantinas and whorehouses were open all night long and the only hardship, other than being there, was riding out each day to patrol the dry dusty roads. They were in search of Pancho Villa and his bandits who on March 9 audaciously attacked Columbus, New Mexico, burning, looting, killing, and they'd been hunting him ever since.

But everywhere they went it was the same story. They just missed them a day ago, an hour ago, the next high valley, the next mountain peak, a cave that did not exist. By most measures the expedition had been a failure.

His brother's job was to turn out as many horses as possible in service to the U.S. Army, while his was to turn out as many horsemen as possible. He took his men out every day and led them over country of all kinds, to teach them every plateau, arroyo, bajada, canyon. He had little faith in their ability and even less in their capacity for improvement.

He remembered Bandy's lips so cracked and blistered it was near impossible for the boy to eat and when he spoke his mouth was too swollen to form words enough to make sense. Every one of them had a case of the piles from so many hard days in the saddle. The seat of Turner's pants was spotted black where they'd bled into the cotton material and would not wash out.

Each morning the red dawn came and all day long was the blazing and deadening heat, but the night could be freezing cold with a swing in temperature of thirty degrees between high noon and midnight.

They wore their peaked Stetsons low on their foreheads and still the light so bright they spent their days squint eyed, or staring through the color-tinted lenses of their goggles. There were wire-framed glasses to purchase: deep green, rose colored, and blue. But there was no blazing corona in the sky to see and only light as if there was no head or brain or mind, but only the idea of light.

He remembered these as the conditions of their lives when they departed expedition headquarters that white chalky morning to hunt the wild beeves. He remembered the morning itself and its dim blue light and upon waking the decision he made to begin another day.

This is what he remembered of those days in Mexico and

much later in life some of it he would talk about, but not everything. He was not inclined to talking, but about these days in the desert, he was even less so.

He remembered a small man, a minor jefe politico, wearing a black felt hat. He was peddling a red hen and a white hen, held by the legs in each hand, and inside the perimeter, down the wind, there were penned and mudded barrow hogs, their flies and their drift of stink.

He remembered a horse trader talking to his brother. Their father had named his brother Xenophon after the ancient horseman and his own name was Napoleon after the great general. Xenophon liked to feed the horses peppermints and the smell of peppermints was constantly on his hands and breath. While he talked to the horse trader, the horses slopped their lips in the trough, their tails idly whisking flies.

From a narrow dirt street there emerged a wedding party, women in summer dresses and men in shirtsleeves, returning home from a long night's celebration. A little wind was moving but not much. Then it concentrated, took a man's straw hat from his head, and disappeared. A water cart trundled by, sprinkling down the dust that would dry and rise again.

He remembered the butchers hooking a team of horses to the hide of a steer they'd slaughtered, slowly dragging the hide off the steer inside out, pearly with tallow and white as snow. The small man wearing the black felt hat, peddling the red hen and the white hen, his jaw working as he watched as the horses tore away the hide.

There was Arbutus, a liquor-head, and from time to time he'd throw himself onto all fours and bark like a rabid dog and he'd howl from the end of his outstretched neck. It was after the dogs were shot Arbutus could be seen dragging a leash with an empty collar and after that he started going down on all fours.

There was the sleeveless baker in his stiff white apron gritted with flour. The baker smoked a cigar he never ashed but let the ash gray and curl and when cold it fell of its own accord. He thought the baker disagreeable and to possess violent proclivities.

There was a goat he remembered and a butcher wearing a bleached-white apron carrying a sticking knife pointed at the sky. The blade gleamed and he caught its light in the corner of his eye. A gaggle of boys followed behind waiting for their chance to lug off the head and guts. Among them was the boy who shined his boots and carried a tin whistle he blew and there was the legless boy strapped to a wheeled platform propelling himself forward with his fists.

And he remembered the chaplain that morning, his joyful greetings and feral sense for all human weakness except his own. He was Protestant, but in Mexico he'd assumed the black cassock, cincture, and a dangling gold crucifix. The people thought him mad for how clamorous his expressions of faith. He descended on the wedding party and snatched a baby from a frightened mother and was lavishing its head with kisses. The mother bowed in fear and held out her hands in supplication, hoping to recover her baby before its soul was eaten. Napoleon did not like the chaplain and suspected him of simony and the selling of indulgences.

And he remembered Preston, a robust young man, his arms and shoulders and neck roped with muscles. Preston wore a very beautiful deerskin jacket that morning, elaborately beaded with long fringe at the sleeves and shoulders. He preferred riding a gray horse with long and rangy legs and that morning was no different. He was urging the photographer to hurry in setting up his camera. He insisted upon a photograph of himself, Stableforth, and Turner on horseback. Preston organized socials and the three wore military cloaks and silver cuff links and all belonged to the same men's club in Delaware. They wore white linen shirts that smelled of eau de cologne and favored flowery bow ties carelessly tied in exploding knots.

The photographer stood at his tripod holding his hat over the lens. The photographer had a habit of setting fires with his flash powder and had managed to burn up a small portion of Mexico.

Why Napoleon consented to such an outlandish request, he had no idea, because for Preston, for what he'd done, he felt only contempt.

A flash went up, an explosion of powder and coming toward him through the rags of smoke was Preston riding the gray.

"What do you want?" Napoleon said before Preston could address him.

"I just want to talk."

"I don't know what I have to say that'd be of any interest."

The others watched their exchange, looking for some sign that might ease the unrest rippling through the camp.

"I apologize for the trouble," Preston said.

"You don't know what trouble is."

"I'd give anything I have to make it not that way."

"You don't know the half of it."

"I'm sorry."

"Don't sorry me," Napoleon said, dismissing the man.

The gray turned and back-stepped and Preston rejoined the men. Napoleon thought to light the cigarette he'd been carrying behind his ear. He put it between his lips. He looked to the sky, a wind-gall. Black disklets floated in his eyes. He closed his eyes and opened them. Today would be weather.

2

THE HORSE NAPOLEON rode that morning was a night-colored stallion called the Rattler horse. It had legs like iron posts. It was known as a hard-mouthed bastard, sharp and difficult rather than easy and lazy, and was blind in one eye so refused to turn on the forehand in that direction, but it didn't matter because it always knew where to go. The horse was able to take a ditch without a spill, clear a wall, leap down a bank at the gallop, or spring up one. It was the very demonstration of impulsion and forward mobility, but was a mean and unforgiving horse.

The first time he mounted the horse it reached back and took his foot in its mouth and dragged him out of the saddle. It was a bitey horse and tried to take a chunk of him. The next time the horse went to bite him he jammed a sizzling beefsteak into its mouth. The horse screamed and lunged from the burn, but it never tried to bite him again.

But on the whole, the Rattler horse was a most absolute and excellent horse. By many accounts the best horse in the army. The horse could start and stop quickly, reverse itself, back up, change directions, stand still when he fired the Springfield and charge at a controlled canter. The Rattler horse was deep chested with a short back, strong haunches, flat legs, a small head and small feet. The horse never lamed, crippled, or galled. The Rattler horse, leaned down to bone, was tireless and unflagging, and his collection of the horse always certain.

On the other hand, his brother rode a succession of mounts. He liked horses with broad short loins because the more easily they collect the hindquarters and lift on the forehand. He believed conformation was behavior and yet, however conformed, they would eventually displease him and go out of favor.

Riding out with him that morning were Extra Billy, Bandy, Preston, Stableforth, and Turner. Extra Billy was named because they already had a Billy when he arrived so he was an extra Billy. He wore a razor scar from ear to chin, a wound he took in the Philippines, back in the day when drunk he cheated at cards. Extra Billy's nose was already bleeding from the dry and heated air.

Extra Billy and Bandy were regular cavalry. Preston, Stableforth, and Turner were all three irregular, America's eager export of losers, deadbeats, cutthroats, dilettantes, and murderers come to Mexico to be part of the hunt for the bandit Pancho Villa. They were the rich and bored gallants. They'd already showed signs of sadism, filing down bullets and hollowing out their points. Now they were half asleep and hung over and as useless to him as tits on a boar hog, with little promise they'd ever be more.

It was last night when word came to him the men were tearing it up and he set out to find them before someone was killed. It wasn't long before he found them in a cantina.

Turner and Stableforth were at a table awash with the light of an oil lamp. They wore wing collars and black silk neckties. They were sitting with two other troopers, Drunk Pete and the German. They were smoking cigars and each had his own bottle of whisky and they had long since dispensed with the use of glasses. They told him they were having a whale of a good time. When he asked after Preston they told him he was in the back with a woman. Drunk Pete was saying how much he loved the army, the rations and liquor being first rate, when there came a summoning scream of pain and horror from the curtains hung at the back. For what reason he did not know, Preston had cut off the woman's ear.

FOOLS LIKE THEM were arriving every day: freebooters, felons, Christians, drifters, patriots. They claimed to be marksmen and veterans of battles no one ever heard of. They were surgeons, mechanics, assassins. Some invented names like Cash McCall, Tennessee Slim, the Kid, Tex, Reverend Joe. In turn, names were invented for them. They were called Fathead, Stupid, Numbnuts. Most were just a bunch of losers and jerk-offs, more trouble than they were worth. They were the future dead, Napoleon thought.

The old soldiers and the young soldiers — both died. They died accidental and intentional. They died from disease and crushing falls. They died from ass-to-hand dysentery. They died from their own horses.

But for Napoleon and his brother, life and death were the same and meant nothing. They'd served from the Indian wars through the Philippines, living in the closed world of the soldier, mistrusting outsiders and only certain of their own, and even then you were obligated to constantly demonstrate your trustworthiness or you were no longer trusted and then you were shunned and driven out. For instance, Arbutus was crazy, but they still trusted him.

As they prepared to ride out that morning there was the distant stuttering of a machine gun gone silent on the firing range as another belt was loaded through the feedlock. The marching band was gathering beneath a shade tarpaulin. Fires blazed in burn pits and the smoke wove above the ground with the stench of the latrines.

He caught sight of his brother again, feeding the horses peppermints. His brother preferred life with the horses, the Negroes, the Apaches. He was a tamer of horses and stayed with the horses and was rarely anywhere but with the horses. His brother loved horses, pleasured in rubbing them down, currying and brushing, and was a sight to behold when witnessed from the ground. He rode with his feet forward and his back and shoulders in perfect arch. Other men stopped to watch him make his pass. He was like a god flying above the earth.

Napoleon loved horses too and the way he and Xenophon sorted through the government horses made them worth their weight in gold. When they first crossed the international line, their horses were fat and indulged, but now their horses were so lean and fit you could see the rippling muscles of their diaphragms. He and his brother, they had no deep feeling for land or people, only horses.

"Hey, Bandy," a trooper named Wheeler yelled. "Kiss my ass."

"You are welcome to go to hell," Bandy yelled back, his words clotted and garbled. Bandy tipped his hat and there followed an exchange of shouted abuse. Wheeler was a loud-mouth and no good and Napoleon had told Bandy to stay clear of him.

Bandy was fair skinned with a rash of freckles across his nose and cheeks. His hair was red as a rooster and in all ways he was vulnerable to the sun. He burned and blistered and suffered heat illness. He tried to keep his lips coated with Vaseline, but was always eating. It seemed the boy ate every-thing he could get his hands on and made him wonder if as a child he'd been starved.

"You covered up good?" Napoleon said. He himself wore a wide neckerchief and slung around his neck were sand gog-gles. His belt was full of ammunition in five-round clips and he carried extra in a bandoleer over his shoulder and another across his saddle, a Springfield rifle fitted with a scope in a saddle boot.

"I am sweating like a pig," Bandy said.

"When you stop sweating is when you're fucked."

"Yessir," the boy replied. He wore a wide-brimmed Stetson and a large square neckerchief, his face only in shadow. He wore long sleeves and stout gloves with a long loose wrist. He claimed to be eighteen years old, but the truth was more like fifteen.

"It's surely gonna be hot today," Bandy said, puffing the words from his mouth.

"Don't talk about it," he said.

"It's gonna be hot enough to put hell out of business."

"What'd I say?"

Bandy knuckled his forehead and begged pardon, but there is so much to remember when you are in the army.

He would have the boy trade wonder for reason, but maybe it was not meant to be.

He stood in his stirrups and twisted around to look back. They were bringing Koons on a stretcher. When he saw Koons his heart tightened. With his right hand he gestured toward his heart the way a superstitious might.

Koons had broken his back in a fall from a horse. They thought him dead when they brought him in so they slung him over his saddle for ten miles, the loose stirrup knocking at his head and mangling his face.

They perched the stretcher handles across sawbucks under a shade tarpaulin. Koons was tall and needed his legs held by a chair. They'd hung mirrors overhead so he could see what was happening. They didn't know what else to do. Being wounded or crippled was worse than death, far worse. The doctor said the trip back north would kill Koons, but sooner or later he'd have to go. Sooner or later they'd all have to go. They couldn't stay in this godforsaken place forever. They'd move on to another country, another war.

Curls of smoke rose from the baker's ovens. He knew the roads and his job was to teach them to these men. But already he was burdened and tired and the day hadn't even begun.

He caught sight of his brother who returned the look as if an intimate of his inner thoughts—what is it?

He shrugged and smiled—nothing.

A flying Jenny buzzed overhead, its pistons firing sporadically. Everyone stopped to watch. Sometimes men shot at the Jenny, said it was something to do, or they said he'd been asking for it.

In an hour the ice wagons would follow to collect the wild beeves. This day would somehow be different, not good, and this feeling he could not escape. He thought the words, begin as you mean to move on.

He nodded to his brother who touched a finger to the brim of his Stetson. He then turned to his men and barked out a command.

Then he clicked his tongue and the Rattler horse stepped off smartly, impatiently, and they were in motion. They formed in column behind him and passed before the files of Sibley tents picketed to the ground, passed through the barb wire and the fixed sentinels at the perimeter.

Behind them the photographer triggered another great flash and rising skyward was a vast cloud of white smoke. Soon their column would be a thin black silhouette quavering in the absolute sunlight.

3

FOR MONTHS THEY'D RIDDEN the stony trails. They'd searched the scattered ranges and barren hills, the dry flat basins, dust and rock to no avail. Every trail they cut was the same story. The bandits were to be found in the next high valley, the next mountain peak, a cave that did not exist. A day ago, an hour ago. The orders they carried were catch in the act and kill on the spot, but the one they sought was as if a wind passed by and his trail ended and cold and all sign disappeared. The bandits knew this broken land and were used to poor food and poor water. They were used to starving.

His brother's work was with the horses and his was to lead men over country of all kinds and to find the bandits. Between them they were to turn out as many cavalrymen as possible in service to the government. But times had changed and this was the new army of the chaplain, the bookkeeper, the teamster, the mechanic, the factotum.

They were entering the rain shadow desert, thousands of square miles that lay between the Sierra Madre Occidentals to the west and the Sierra Madre Orientals to the east. Briefly it had been wet, but now it was dry and rainless and had been for several weeks and what was green and lush and overrich had lost its verdancy and was now desiccated and the memory of one made no difference to the experience of the other.

"Give those horses breathing space," he commanded, and each paused until the distance lengthened and they strung along the trail and the only sound was the silent lift and hushed fall of shod hooves.

Bandy rode behind and then Preston, Stableforth, Turner, and Extra Billy in the rear. Extra Billy was most dependable when sober, though he had a talent for sleeping in the saddle, his eyes wide open.

Often Napoleon looked back to the light rising behind them, the sun seeming to resize each new moment, the land shredding into gold, and there was nothing to be seen but weltering shimmer and tangle of glitter and the dazzle inside his eye.

A voice in his head kept telling him something would happen today.

He felt the sweat trickling inside his collar. He thought by now he was so old and dried up to be incapable of sweat, even when bathed in heat inescapable. Already the horses' hides were shining with sweat. He skimmed the Rattler's neck and snapped the sweat from his fingers. However ill tempered and unmanageable the horse, its backbone was sunk deep and riding the horse was more pleasant than sitting or standing.

His mind went to the place of thought. He'd long passed the middle life and now faced the last of his years. He thought how a man reaches an age where he's done a lot and when he looks back he can see it all. He sees what he's done and can't imagine doing as much in the years to come.

He felt a momentary trembling and recoil of the Rattler horse beneath him, so complete had their minds become.

His father once told him the day has eyes and the night has ears. He looked back to find the hazy rim made by earth and sky, the barren, borderless, and immense world they'd come to, its fearful and consoling emptiness. The wind was increasing and their dust signature drifted behind them. The still puffs seemed to bloom and fall where they rose, but they did not. The blossoms traveled. There was something different. It drew on his mind and try as he might he could not figure it out.

"It's the wind," he said to himself. "The wind has switched."

For months the prevailing winds came from the east. But the wind had changed directions and was now coming from the west.

"That ain't all," the voice said. It was a woman's voice he heard and the Rattler horse scissored its ears.

He turned in his saddle, half expecting the column vanished, but they were still there, plodding the cracked and calcined earth, drowsy and dodgy, still drunk and about asleep in the saddle.

The expedition had become a stage for so many men to play out their ambitions and imaginations. Preston was tall and young and his was a handsome face. He was lean and still weighed two hundred pounds and was strong through his legs and chest and arms. He had blond hair he wore parted in the middle and greased to the sides where it curled. He was in the first part of being young and comported himself as if immortal. He was from Maryland and often spoke of sailing on the Chesapeake. An avid gambler and consistently unlucky at dice and cards, he owed debts to many of the men and some amounts were not insignificant. He really was a boy and not a man. He was a boy grown up but still not a man.

Riding behind Preston was Stableforth, bright eyed and pink cheeked and attempting a mustache. On the whole, a good stout-hearted fellow, but a scientist, he had no business being where he was.

Next was Turner, who was artistic. He carried pencils, watercolors and brushes, a tablet of paper, and also had no business being where he was.

The three were well fitted, their kit tailored and custom made in Baltimore and London. They were warrior princes who presumed lions in their blood, and having killed a trophy hall of wild animals, they were hunting their first man killing, preferably without much fall of their own blood.

When Preston spoke, which was often, his stories were too earnest to be bragging and too fantastic to be lies and were corroborated by Stableforth and Turner. In the presence of his superiors he exhibited extravagant manners and cloying deference and was liked for how exaggerated his person. He talked unabashedly about becoming a senator one day.

The three of them together spoke of France with mystery and fascination: the machine gun, the flamethrower, the gas. He could not deny them the seductive power of violence. They spoke of the war as if the new God. He didn't know if they'd get their taste; he supposed they would and he wished for them everything they wanted, the poison and fire, the mud and gut shreds, the invisible streams of lead.

Napoleon didn't hate anyone, because he didn't particularly care about anyone enough to hate them. But for these men he held slight regard and for Preston he felt only disdain.

He looked back again and Preston smiled, a tight line his mouth, and touched a gloved finger to the brim of his Stetson. He made no gesture in reply and turned his back to the man. Sooner or later he'd have to be dealt with.

4

MIDMORNING THE SKY was blue and shot with spears of light. They came to a rail bed bordering a wide, arid, waterless basin. The rails continued on, winding the mountainside before disappearing into a tunnel. Beneath, the broad plain was covered by sage and mesquite, and crossing it was a tiny figure the field glasses revealed to be an old man leading a mule loaded with pick and pan as well as minimum and necessary provisions.

Napoleon told them to stay put and pointed the Rattler horse toward the old man. He pressed with his legs and light in hand, the Rattler horse crossed the tracks to where the trail bent and fell in switchbacks to the desert floor.

He dismounted and called to the old man. Startled, the old man looked up. A whirlwind ginned and skittered across the desert grassland. A jag of wolf lightning descended from the clear blue sky.

The old man worked his way up through the light pulling a short lead rope attached to the mule's halter ring. He wore blue denim overalls, an overshirt to match, and a coat stitched from canvas. His other hand was wrapped in a dirty rag. He grew in the shimmer, huffing up the last rise to stand beside him.

He'd heard rumors the man was down here prospecting the last unexplored mountains on the continent. He couldn't remember when last he'd seen him. Nevada, the Dakotas—he could not remember.

But now, he did not look well. It was more than age and the grim life he lived in the rough wild. There was a smell he carried, of decay.

The mule, roach backed and broken winded, brayed three great honking noises and then went silent. The mule's ears were tatters and in its head was one fixed eye and one loose sclerotic eye. Its neck was skinny and its legs no more than spindles. The Rattler horse nickered and shook its head, rattling the bit in its mouth and scattering froth, wanting away from the stench of these two.

The old man removed his hat to wipe the sweat from his forehead. His red nose was sketched with broken vessels and his dirty gray beard hung down to his chest. He was toad eyed with black and sagging eye pouches and wore a ragged neck cloth, stiff with salt. He rubbed at the swelled veins in his temples and then gave a phlegmy cough that doubled him over. In the east the sun-whitened sky had darkened and there was walking rain. The old man stood gazing into the sky, his bandaged hand clasped behind his back. It'd been months since last it rained and they watched it step cross the land and disappear.

"What are you doing out here?" the old man finally said. "Haven't you got enough sense to get out of the sun?"

"There's always one more war to fight."

"After the war is before the war," the old man said, his expansive forehead glistening with newly sprung sweat.

"I never did plan on dying of old age."

"You and me both," the old man said. He thrust a finger into his ear hole and gave it a jiggle.

"It's been an age since last I saw you," Napoleon said. "You have lasted."

"Yes. I have lasted," the old man said.

"The last time I saw you," he started to say, but couldn't finish the sentence.

"It was quite a long time ago. Since the war I never know what day it is."

"The mind is a funny thing."

"Where's your brother?" The old man raised his feathery eyebrows as if the question was a delight.

"Back that way," he nodded. "He's lasted too."

"I been down south," the old man said.

"Were it bad down there?"

"Bad enough."

"That bad," he sighed.

"Have you got anything to smoke?"

"Baccy."

The old man unwrapped a meerschaum pipe from a rag. It had a curved stem and a silver lid. There was a tremble in his hands he could not control.

"How far you think you been?"

"Since when?" the old man said.

"Since you started?"

"Thirty thousand miles give or take a thousand miles."

"That's a far way."

"I saw them shoot Maximillian."

"My grandfather was here in 'forty-six. And my father after him."

"There's a lot to remember in life and too much to forget," the old man said, packing his pipe with what he did not spill. "One gets tired after seeing so much."

"What have you seen today?" Napoleon asked, striking him a match.

"You got yourself tangled up in a civil war," the old man said, accepting the match.

"I hear that."

"I did too one time. Life's a hard school."

The old man drew the soporific smoke deep into his lungs. With his bandaged hand he swabbed the perspiration from his face before he spoke.

"Where'd you find this mean bastard?" the old man said of the Rattler horse.

"Come down from up north. Montana. Wyoming. I don't really know."

"You'll never get to the bottom of that horse."

"No, I don't believe I will."

"How long you been out here?"

"Since day broke."

The old man nodded and his eyes were as if he'd lost the thread of conversation.

"What do you see?"

"Today?" the old man said. "Why, the devil's out today."

The old man closed his eyes and made vague gestures as if infested with the invisible and each time he did he set the air with his stench.

"How many is riding with him?"

"Him who?"

"Him the devil."

"He's enough. He'll set death on you all by himself."

"He's trouble that way."

"He's a deceiving bastard."

"Are you hungry?" Napoleon said, the old man's news settling in his mind.

"Not that I know of," the old man said. His mouth was lathered in white foam and there was a crust at the corners.

"I'm so hungry I could eat the asshole out of a skunk."

"Yes, I am hungry then too."

He led the old man to where the others waited and they could smell him too. They shared with him their biscuit and canned meat. Below them the broken land simmered beneath the hot sun. He found for the old man a can of tuna fish and cut it open. As the old man slurped from the can, fish oil ran from his lips and disappeared into his chin whiskers. He finished off the can and then turned his head and spit in the dust.

"Do you have any coconut pie?" the old man inquired, and they all laughed. Then a change came over him and he told them he had to keep going and hastened to continue on his way without so much as a nod, but he didn't get far before he staggered and fell, his face awash in sweat and fever. He rolled to his side and began vomiting the tuna and biscuit and canned meat.

Napoleon went down on one knee beside the old man where he lay in the dirt and touched his shoulder.

"You going to let me look inside that rag?" he asked.

The old man fixed his eyes on him and said, "I shall be grateful if you would." He raised his hand the way a dog would raise its paw.

Beneath the dirty windings the old man's index finger was black and purplish blue. The skin was split and shriveled. The fingernail was gone and the finger swollen and the discharge was violent to Napoleon's senses. The old man told how he crushed the finger some days ago. The wound had turned angry and the hurt was fearsome, but now he could feel it very little.

"Gangrene," Stableforth intoned from over his shoulder.

He touched the old man's forehead. He was burning with fever. He helped the old man shuck his canvas coat and with his folding knife he opened the sleeve of the old man's over-shirt. Inside his sleeve the old man's arm was freckled and goose-white and a faint green streak ran up his forearm. The old man saw it too and closed his eyes in resignation.

Napoleon bent forward and laid his hand carefully upon the old man's shoulder, and in the touch was their understanding. The old man raised his head slowly and his fear-bright eyes did not waver. They both knew what must happen.

Napoleon told the men he needed their canteens, a piece of soap, the nippers from the horseshoeing outfit. In his bags he found a shirt, a razor and the bottles of medicine he carried. He opened the nippers and with a stone whetted the blades.

"Start a fire," he said, handing them to Turner, "and burn them."

"Give him your bottle," he said to Extra Billy who made no argument.

Napoleon wet his hands and soaped them and then he scrubbed the old man's stained and dirty hand, but he could not change what the earth and sun had done. He washed the old man's arm and then his own hands again while the old man drank from Extra Billy's bottle, his gangrenous arm propped on a rock.

When Turner handed him the red hot nippers, he nodded and the men stepped forward to take hold of the old man's shoulders.

"Git yore god damn hands off me," the old man cried.

"Let him have his own way," he told them, and when they stepped back Napoleon suddenly forced the handles together and the rotted finger fell away from where it joined the hand.

The old man groaned and gave a galvanic start. He held up his hand and looked at it with astonishment. His lip began to tremble. Then his eyes rolled upwards and only the whites were visible. He sighed deeply and collected himself for what was next.

"Whisky him," he said, and Extra Billy allowed the old man another long pull from the bottle and the old man told him he was ready.

With the razor he laid open the green streak in the old man's forearm and drenched it with a purgation. He dressed the wound with shirting saturated in carbolic acid, the solution hissing and bubbling.

"It's time you harbored," he said to the old man.

The old man's eyes soured and then they blazed. Then he said, "Some of us, we are condemned to endure life."

"Ain't you the wise owl," Napoleon said.

He lit the old man's pipe for him and rolled himself a ciga-rette he placed behind his ear. He told the old man there'd be wagons shortly and if he knew what was good for him he'd hitch a ride.

5

THEY PULLED THEMSELVES into the saddles and turned onto the road bordering the rail bed. The old man slept in the shade of a shelter cloth with water and food. He'd done the best he could do. God knows he'd endured like experiences, if not worse, and too long he'd dallied with doctoring. He could not allow himself anymore distractions.

He stepped the Rattler horse along the edge of the dull tracks, swiveled in the saddle, and looked back into the shimmering emptiness. He stopped and waited and there came the shriek of an engine, the clang of a bell, and soon the clatter of the car wheels on the tracks began to sing.

The locomotive pushed a flat car with machine gunners whose uniforms he did not recognize. Then came the locomotive, the tender, the train faster now, the couplings rattling violently. Then was a hiss of steam and the rushing chain of iron and steel as if released and the wheels clacking and hammering the grade. Sparks and ballast flew as if not a train but a war machine whose travel was confined to flat steel rails.

Sunlight flashed through the swift openings, the wooden freight cars, black coaches, the knock of the wheels clipping over the rail joints the sound of clacking dominoes. More soldiers rode on the roofs of the cars, rocking to the train's spasmodic motion. They did not wave, their staring eyes black as obsidian and there were armed men on the platforms staring down at him, rifle barrels dull in the clipping shadows. They were men in black broadcloth suits, American gunmen hired onto someone's payroll.

The Rattler tossed its head and shifted impatiently.

A face in the train turned to look at him through a window. There was an instant of recognition and then it turned to streaking shadow and disappeared quick as thought. The train curved away and grew smaller and smaller. Its squat funnel disappeared. Its caboose disappeared and then it was swallowed in the distance by the tunnel. He listened to its shunting echoes and then there was silence again on the plain and his hearing retuned.

The smell of smoke and hot burnt steel was left in the train's wake and down the line a sun-whited hacienda suddenly came into view as if freight delivered from the boxcars.

They followed the road for several miles where they passed through the walls of the hacienda. The buildings were low and rectangular, peeling plaster and decaying adobe. Inside the walls was a square and a dry fountain and atop a pedestal was the Virgin Mother. There was the statue of a little boy sitting with his knees drawn to his chest and held clasped in his arms. There was a birdcage with the bones of small dead birds. There were empty flower beds and cracked and tumbled basins as if time was a gentle hand. Dried cornstalks were scraping in a sprung breeze. He could hear them and then their sound stopped. From deep inside the warren of rooms came the sound of water in the darkness trickling into a basin. In the pens were white skeletons, gnawed bones sticking out of the rubble, and beyond were dead fields and a dying orchard.

The ground rose and then abruptly and soon they were threading a single track higher and higher. The unbearable heat throbbed against Napoleon's body and then his lower back began to ache sharply. Increasingly he felt an urgency and to be done with this detail. The Rattler, its two ears cocked, started and quivered.

"What is it?" he whispered. "What is it?"

They followed the broken path beneath a wide-spreading shelf of rock and just when the trail petered out they came to a trickle of water and a patch of green. In the valley distant he anticipated the wild beeves and sure enough through the field glasses, he could see them from the rim. They stopped to allow the horses to drink and to tighten the clinches on their horseshoes. Napoleon dabbed at the cool water with his finger. Then he cupped the water and drank from his palm. He took a second drink and then rinsed his face and neck.

After they watered and rested he took Bandy and Preston down a path through the rocks, careful not to disturb the grazing animals.

"Bang. Bang," Preston whispered, looking down on the beeves' black shapes.

"They won't be hard to kill from here," Bandy said.

"It ain't killing them what's hard," Napoleon said. "We could have kilt them from the rim."

"What's so hard then?"

"What's hard is getting them out of there once they have been shot."

"What's the matter?" Bandy said.

"I don't know," he said, irritated the boy should intrude on his private deliberations. Then, before he could stop himself, he said, "Something ain't right."

"What is it?"

"I said I don't know.

"But something."

"Do you see something?" Preston asked, but how could he explain he was trying to see something beyond the range of the naked eye? How could he say he was trying to see a feeling he had? How to say, all is told and there is nothing unknown. It is simply yet to be revealed.

"Quit your yammering," he told them. "I said, I don't know, god dammit."

Down below, the beeves began to move as he knew they would. He slid away from the rocks and the two men followed. They went back to the trickle of water, collected their horses, and rode to the top of the range. Then they crawled on hands and knees to a ridge where the beeves could not see them in the rocks or wind them on the air. The beeves were still a mile away and were moving higher and in their direction, but they could not see them yet.

They waited and soon the beeves appeared, scrawny range cattle, but if spooked their lumbering bodies were capable of running like antelope.

"They'll be tougher than Zip's ass," Napoleon said, snugging the butt of the Springfield to his shoulder.

"Who's Zip?" Bandy whispered.

"How the hell do I know who Zip is. It's a saying," he hissed.

"Zip's ass," Bandy said, trying it out for himself.

Grazing beyond a thick band of creosote were the cows with their young and the vigilant bulls among them. He counted fifteen, five large, and stopped counting. The beeves had suddenly became uneasy. They were aware of a presence. He sniffed at the wind—rising and coming in. Why so uneasy?

He steadied in position and inside the eye of the prismatic scope he found the sight picture he wanted. He calculated three hundred yards. He set the range to correspond and placed his aiming point a little behind the shoulder blade and two-thirds down from the spine, a heart shot. The box magazine held five rounds. Breathing calmly, he squeezed the trigger and fired, absorbing the shock and feeling the grind in his shoulder.

He immediately adjusted the sight picture. The cross-hairs found their spot and another bull crumpled. A cow turned to look at the bull when it groaned. Then the cow fell, the shot breaking her neck when she looked up. A fourth cow began running, jinked left and went down, skidding nose first in the red dirt.

At the fifth report the herd hared off in a single curving direction. Their bony pitching bodies closed with the ground as their strides lengthened and dodged for safety. Five times he'd squeezed the trigger and the five large animals fell.

"Bravo," Preston shouted, punching the air with his fist.

He waited until Extra Billy, Stableforth, and Turner rode out with knives to bleed the carcasses and only then did he sit up and pass the Springfield to Bandy who cradled it in his arms. He was starting to feel twitchy in the heat. He surveyed the surround, his eyes half closed to see better.

Bandy was holding out a canteen of water. He heard words. The boy was talking to Preston.

"Wheeler says there was a soldier who died at Fort Yuma and went to hell only to come back for his blanket. Ask me why."

"Why?" Preston said.

"Because it was too cold down there in hell and I'd say right now it is hotter than Yuma ever was."

"Over there," Napoleon said and pointed to a dusty mountain pass. "We'll get in there for the noon spell."

He'd rest the men and the weary horses and perhaps a few moments of sleep for himself. Soon the wagons would come along. He'd chip ice to melt inside his mouth.

He told them to direct the others to follow and then rode into the blind spot where the trail was so thin there was not room to turn a horse around. On the other side the trail descended into a little box canyon, more an empty column of stone, where it wasn't so bad a place to spend some time.

He knew the place well. He'd been there before, a place where there was a dry falls and water jetting from a port in the rock face, and at the base of the dry falls a series of water tanks, one lipping into the next. The bottom ones were full of sand, but higher up there was water. There was an alcove with ancient artwork and handprints made from blown paint. The last time he was there pollen was floating in the tank.

6

BY THE TIME the others rode in Napoleon had unsaddled the Rattler horse. He told the horse to lie down and it rolled in the sand as if a great cheerful dog. He then yelled, Hup! and it scrambled to its feet where it shook and stood sheepishly for how undignified its display. It blinked its eyes as if shy and abashed and not the malevolent it truly was.

"Tend to your horses first," he ordered them. "Then wash your faces and change your socks."

The day only half over and already he was bone weary.

"Eat your food," he said. He had to teach them how to live. He had to teach them how not to get killed by their own irresponsible behavior.

"If you're pissin' dark you need water," he told them, and still they would get into trouble, not even smart enough to read their own piss.

He took off his boots and soaked his feet in the same water he washed his socks and then wrung them out. Their work done, there was now time. He let down his pants and rubbed his aching knees with an embrocation that smelled like turpentine. His knees went hot and then cold. He let the air take away the fumes before pulling his pants onto his hips. He put on another pair of socks and his boots and the wet socks he lashed to his saddle.

In his ditty bag he had a fat red apple, some dried beef and biscuit.

He lay back, folded his hands under his armpits and closed his eyes. When next he looked, they were gathered around Stableforth, peering at the something he held in his hand. It was a scorpion flexing its long tail. Stableforth tipped his hand and let it walk onto a stone where, crablike, it scuttled from sight.

"Stableforth says this were all a inland sea at one time." It was Bandy talking from the midstream of his thoughts, the boy's mind escaping his mouth.

On the high ground was Extra Billy, scanning the rocks and then looking his way. Napoleon gestured with an open palm — do you see anything? Extra Billy shook his head.

"He says you can tell from the kind of dirt and what's underneath the dirt," Bandy was saying.

"How's he know what's underneath the dirt?" Napoelon said. "Has he ever been there?"

He could see the peak of Extra Billy's Stetson bob once and a second time and then disappear.

"I don't know," the boy said. "I didn't think to ask."

"Well, maybe next time you ought to before you go and tell everyone."

"Wheeler says Preston's got a map to a lost Spanish silver mine."

"I told you to stay clear of Wheeler?"

"He don't like you much either," the boy said.

If it wasn't gold it was silver. If it wasn't silver it was copper.

What man in this army didn't claim to be in possession of a map, or know of a map, or have faith in the existence of such a map?

"What's the matter now?" he asked the boy.

"I am still a boy to them."

"You are a boy," he said.

"Wal' then you can go to hell too."

"Do you know the way?"

"If there is better directions than you already have then I will let you know."

He offered the boy a thin slice of apple from his knife blade. The boy took it and with his eyes closed he eased it into his mouth. His nose was bleeding from the heat and he took in his own blood with the apple slice.

He told the boy his nose was bleeding and to rub Vaseline inside his nostrils. The boy wiped his nose on his sleeve, smearing blood across face.

"Go wash your face," Napoleon said.

Extra Billy was returning from the bush, buttoning his trousers. He liked Extra Billy. He was hard headed and as he drank enough liquor for three men he probably drank too much. It was his habit to drink himself sober and then get drunk all over again and the drunker he became the more sober and improved he appeared.

"That boy would eat a pig's ass if he had to," Extra Billy said.

"You got bottle fever without your bottle?"

Extra Billy hooked one thumb in his armpit and rocking on his heels, he looked away to the distance in front of him.

"I point-blank asked you a question," Napoleon said, but

still there was no reply. "Feeling the bottom?" he said more gently.

"Yessir, the bottom."

"The bottom bottom?"

"Still the top bottom."

"Do me a favor?"

"What?"

"Watch the boy."

"Mister in-one-ear-and-out-the-other?"

"He's a trier."

Rising up and down on the balls of his feet, Extra Billy shrugged — whatever.

"You drunk right now?"

"Nossir."

"You ain't lying?"

"Nossir. Swear to God," Extra Billy said, and crossed his heart.

"What's the matter with you then?"

"I feel like I'm pissing porcupines."

"Something out there?"

Extra Billy made a sour face and shrugged — something.

"Best get to the doc when we return."

"Sir," Extra Billy then said, taking off his Stetson and holding it by its curled brim with both hands.

"Speak up."

"Did you ever think of getting married?"

"I ain't jumping into any ocean, if that's what you mean."

"I was just asking."

"I never looked for any woman to make me happy."

"I was just asking."

"Well, I have never been asked that type of question before."

"I was thinking about it."

"You had surely better see the doc then."

"Yessir," Extra Billy said, and directionless he shuffled off.

Bandy returned to his side. He'd scrubbed his face and there was color showing in his cheeks. His lips and nostrils he'd lubricated with Vaseline and they shined.

"Does he ever say if I'm doing okay?" Bandy said.

"Who?"

"Who do you think? Your brother." The boy had recently experienced a severe dressing-down from his brother. While practicing sword work on horseback he'd managed to cut the ears off a horse. Cutting the ears off a horse in mounted sword exercise or battle was not unusual; you just didn't do it when Xenophon was your instructor.

"If you weren't doing all right he'd let you know."

"I don't think he likes me."

"Well, son. He's often unfriendly to people he likes. He ignores me completely," and to this the boy made a bashful grin.

He looked into the sun and his eyes filled with tears from the light and he wiped them away. He refocused his eyes. From somewhere came a bounce of light, as if the sun was being dazzled with a mirror.

"Did you see that?" he asked.

"What?'

"Nothing," he said, shaking his head.

He then asked the boy if he'd changed his socks and when the boy said he did he told him to get up where Extra Billy had been, to stay out of sight, to see and not be seen, and the boy obeyed.

He rolled a cigarette and reclined against the curve of a dished boulder and let his eyes close. He slowed his breathing and his heart softened and it wasn't long before he could hear his own blood.

"Sir, permission to speak." He started against the rock, his right hand to the .45 he carried in a shoulder rig. It was Preston, a hand at his chin, waiting to speak.

"Quit the preamble and state your business," he said, dusting cigarette ashes from his shirtfront.

"If a thing comes into my head, I just have to say it."

"That's good to know."

"I have a weakness for pretty girls."

"All men do."

"Last night I drank too much and I threw up. I embarrassed myself."

"That ain't all you did."

"Before you judge me, do you know everything that happened?"

"I know enough."

"What do you know?"

"I know you shouldn't ought to have cut that girl."

"You hold it against me what happened, but I tell you she was stealing my money."

"I surely don't want to listen to all your puke," he said, adjusting the brim of his Stetson. He could not believe how incredible this one. Last night when he found him he was drunk and the woman's blood was saturating the little bed where she'd taken him behind the curtain.

"I am not a bad man," Preston said as he toed the dirt with his boot.

"I don't care if you're the pope of Rome. You're lucky I don't stick a knife in you right now."

"Give me another chance. Please."

"Is that what you're used to?" he said, but to this Preston had no reply. He folded his arms across his chest and with one foot in front of the other, he stared down at the ground.

Napoleon closed his eyes and opened them and cast them to the high rocks where Bandy was, the crown of his Stetson in view.

"I know someone by what they say and do, " Napoleon finally said.

"But a man doesn't know what he's doing when he's drunk."

"Right now I just wish you'd shut the fuck up."

"Don't hold it against me is what I am asking."

"I ain't the one with reason for to hold a grudge."

Bandy raised his head and grinned down at him. Napoleon held open a hand—okay? Bandy nodded and lowered his head again.

He understood how Preston could not accept his rebuke. Approval and forgiveness were the right and habit of this man's station in life. What he did was done.

Napoleon wanted this conversation over. He made it a rule to stay away from people who talked too much and this one was a talker. Today they were all talkers and he'd about had enough of their talk. Then Preston was talking again.

"I am simply asking you to please don't hold it against me." Preston had worked himself up and his color was showing in his cheeks. In his way he'd confessed his role in what happened last night. He must have thought, what more could he do? When one confesses, forgiveness is required.

"Did you pay for your hump?" he said.

"What?" Preston said, his voice a quaver.

"Did you pay for your hump," he said again, but Preston only stared at him, a young man's thin tight smile on his face. By the look in his eyes it was clear he'd struggled with his behavior and failed before.

"I was off my head," Preston declared. "When we return I will make restitution." Preston then said he needed to take a short walk to concentrate his mind that he might recover the day and with that he dismissed himself.

"What's up with Mister Moneybags?" Extra Billy asked.

"He ain't nothing but a poisonous tick," Napoleon said.

"He ain't so bad."

"He ain't so good either."

"A whore getting cut up happens."

"You defending it?"

"I ain't defending nothing."

"You know what he done as well as I do cuttin' that woman."

"I know what he done. You ain't telling me nothing."

"He ought to be horsewhipped. Do around me what that man did and you will rue the day."

"Him horsewhipped? Why, he's going to be a senator some day. He was created by God, that one."

"All the more reason."

"The kid," Extra Billy said. "I talked to him like you said."

"What about him?"

"He don't understand why we are here."

"What'd you tell him?"

"I tol' him the army is here and he is in the army and that's why he is here. But that other one."

"Who?'

"Preston."

"What about him?"

Extra Billy turned his palms to the sky and gave a shrug and he likewise dismissed himself.

Napoleon lit a new cigarette off the one he'd been smoking.

Don't try to understand, he told himself. What seemed so strange and impenetrable earlier in the day seemed to have vanished, but his heart beat uneasily with the sense they should be moving. It pressed on his mind. He tired of his cigarette. He crumbled and scattered it away.

He closed his eyes for not more than a few minutes, when there came a commotion from the rocks. Preston and Turner were whooping and dancing backward as Stableforth pulled a nesting rattlesnake, thick as a man's arm, from a wide crevice. He held it aloft by the throat as its body twisted and flashed white in the air. Its fanged mouth yawed open and its tongue slivered the air.

Turner held open a flour sack and once the snake was inside they tied off the sack and dropped the sack into another and then a third. This was their adventure and they would have it.

He looked to the sun. The wagons would be coming in with their blocks of ice. Their make-work detail would soon be over and he'd be rid of them.

"Let's get cracking," Napoleon said.

He pulled himself erect and dusted himself off. He walked into the bush and unbuttoned his fly. As he was doing his business he scanned the jagged rocks that rimmed the canyon, the hour just past the meridian. There was nothing to see and then suddenly a flash of arc-shaped light in the periphery of his vision and to the west, he caught sight of distant riders, one a woman with a parasol, passing ghostlike through the vast emptiness.

The devil ain't a man, he thought. He's a woman.

He watched them as they disappeared beneath the earth line. He didn't know who they were, but they were familiar to him, as if prefigured in his mind. There would be trouble; he now knew it and with this knowing, some small part of him was relieved.

7

H E STARED INTENTLY through the heat haze. There'd been a movement on the horizon, a vague outline of horses and riders. It went away and then he saw it again. How far? In this country you could see a campfire twenty-five miles away.

A nerve was twitching in his cheek. He lifted the field glasses from his chest to see if they revealed anything his eyes could not. His nostrils flared as if to learn what rode the dead heated air. He adjusted the wheel and swept the barren sun-struck rim, but there was only dazzling light and empty infinite white sky. Black ashlike floaters within the round of his eyeball crossed his sight line. They drifted and then they settled.

Extra Billy was standing at his elbow, the smell of sweated liquor a heat on his skin.

"Speak your mind," Napoleon said, the field glasses still trained on the far-off rim of the canyon wall.

"There's riders out there," Extra Billy said, his voice a whisper so as not to be heard by the others. "But I trust you already know that."

"I do."

The black floaters multiplied. They crossed his retina again and settled from his line of sight to the bottom of his eye. The future appeared to him in a brief burst. It left behind no particular event or detail of event, but for an instant it was there in his mind and it was terrible and he felt weakened.

"You think they're friendly?" Extra Billy said.

"If we don't know them, they ain't friendly," he said, letting his hand to flex open and the gesture restored him, but he still remembered his fear.

"What do you think their business is?"

"I don't know what their business is. What do you think?"

"Playing guess-the-number. Trying to figure how many of us there is."

"Maybe."

"Where are those fucking wagons?"

"Not here."

"What are we going to do?"

For the last hour the watchful Rattler horse had been nervous and now he knew why, or rather his mind understood what it already knew. They were not the only riders in the sun-whited country this day. There were others. They had remained below the horizon line the whole time, but the Rattler horse knew they were there.

"What is it?" Bandy had joined them and wanted to know. His mouth was full of crackers and a scumble of biscuit crumbs were clotted in the Vaseline that rounded his swollen lips.

Napoleon told Bandy to pay attention to the horses. He told the boy that horses are prey animals. The way their eyes are set in their heads affords them a very broad vision. They will spot and they will run away. Though he was not as committed to the intelligence of horses as his brother, he easily conceded the superiority of a horse's mind to that of a human being's.

"Right now," he told Bandy, "we might likewise be prey animals."

"I never thought of it that way."

"Just what do you think a horse sees when it looks at you?" he asked. He let down the field glasses and turned on the boy.

"I don't know," the boy said.

"Another god damn horse," Extra Billy said, and spit in the dust at his feet.

Napoleon raised the field glasses again and saw them a second time. Two riders broke into sight and disappeared just as quickly. They wore wide-brimmed hats and carried rifles slung across their backs. They were not the same riders as he'd seen before. There was the woman again. She rode stiffly and carried a parasol. Her equipment flashed brilliantly with sunlight. Silver, he thought, and how many of her was there? That made as many as six riders. He knew if there was six, there could just as easily be sixty. He did not know who they were but knew they were the answer to the riddle of this day.

"I got no patience for a fight today," Napoleon said, as if bored by the prospect of an encounter. There was no reason to convey the alarm that dogged his mind.

"This land ain't worth the devil coming to fetch it away," Extra Billy said. "Much less fight for it."

"Do we make a stand here?" Bandy asked.

"No, you fool. We get the fuck out of here," Extra Billy said.

"Do you think we'll have a fight?"

"I hope to God we don't," Napoleon said. The last thing he wanted to do was go into battle with the men he'd drawn that morning. Extra Billy would serve him well. Of this he was confident, but the rest were too green and untested.

"Why not?" Bandy wanted to know.

"Because we will be kilt," Extra Billy said, and laughed as if the idea of it made him a little bit insane.

They smoothed their blankets and lifted their saddles. They hauled tight on the cinches, mounted up and they left the little box canyon. They rode slowly at first as they negotiated the thin trail and then they rode hard from the place where they had harbored.

There was still no sign of the wagons.

They descended the thin stony trail and broke out onto the valley floor, but the beeves they shot and bled an hour ago had vanished. There was no trace of them to be found, no blood, no hoof, no worthless guts and this eventually convinced Preston, Stableforth, and Turner that there was danger. At first they thought they'd been robbed and they were outraged that such could happen. The beeves were their own and they wanted justice, but when there was only silence from the others, they quieted, their minds unnerved.

He lifted the field glasses and scanned the vast emptiness of the broken country. But he didn't need to. The Rattler horse was vibrating with the news of their surroundings and who occupied them. Then he saw them. The distant riders had multiplied and placed themselves between him and the direction he intended. He caught sight of them as if miniature points on the compass of their world. They knotted the landscape in twos and threes. They were to the north and the east and the west and to the south a speck of a man holding a rifle stood over the thin trail they'd just descended and then a second man stepped from the rocks and stood beside him. They appeared and disappeared in the shimmering glaze of heat, as if ink drawn and washed away and drawn again.

"Who could they be?" Turner said.

Napoleon let the field glasses to his chest and spoke harshly to the Rattler horse that it ought to be ashamed for its demonstration and should compose itself in a more befitting way. He explained to the men their situation as he understood it and his intention that they should extricate themselves as best as was possible.

"We should attack," Preston declared. "Only the offensive is decisive."

Extra Billy said that he should shut his g.d. mouth for once, wanting no intrusion on the thoughts of Napoleon.

Napoleon waved off Extra Billy and pointed at Preston as if to fix him in place. "Having the advantage," he said to him, "is better than impulse, and right now they have the advantage."

He told them they would travel in a violent hurry. He touched with his heels and pressed with his legs and the Rattler horse was spurred into effortless motion. He left them behind to catch up and one by one they did, leaving the stony plain of saltbush and creosote and they rode from the valley floor, their numbers strung out to let the horses breathe, no matter how inclined the animals were to herd with the leader.

Napoleon's mind incandesced. Where did he go wrong and how would he make amends? He worked his mind over again and again. Were the beeves the bait and while they rested in the little box canyon the trap sprung? He'd passed this way before when he first saw the beeves and he'd rested in the same little box canyon that same day at the height of the sun. One repetition. Two repetitions. That would have been enough. Where he'd made his mistake was right here and he'd made it days ago. The only question left to be answered was, who would pay for that mistake?

He touched at the Rattler horse to widen the distance between it and Preston's gray. The horse opened up and stretched for length and behind him the other horses fell back and then they recovered and ran on the Rattler horse, having no other mind than to be with it and afraid of being lost without it.

He guided for what seemed a flank, a notched pass in the mountain's saddle, but the distant riders had their own intentions and one of them was not to give up a flank. They broke for the notch and were cleared and began their descent, but at each turn there were men lying in wait. They stood and aimed their rifles and he veered off, but for some reason they did not take the shots they were afforded.

When he held up to collect and turn the Rattler horse, it tossed its head and nickered and he chastised it this time for making such wanton sound. The horse pranced about and shook its face. The Rattler was game and fearless, but he knew this cat-and-mouse could not last forever, and he also knew that when you are the mouse you don't have much to say about it to the cat.

Preston rode in first, his gray already blown and exhausted. Again he suggested their proper course was to attack.

Napoleon called down his nerves and blood. He gave to Preston a scornful look: what do you know about such business? This is their hunting ground and right now we are the hunted. He thought to say these words but kept them to himself. He did not know if this was a day that would be marked by death, but he knew they were in for more than he'd anticipated and he knew the odds were swiftly changing in death's favor. He told Preston they could stand anytime, but for now they would run. He allowed him that much of his thinking.

The others rode in one by one, Bandy, Stableforth, and Turner, and stood nervous and jostling. In their eyes was confusion, exhilaration, and panic. The Rattler horse glared wildly and started backwards. It wanted to keep running.

He looked at the green men he rode with. Maybe on this day, a day full of ill omen, maybe at last something was happening in their lives. He knew they were trying to think about ways to think and he knew they were thinking about fear. If not, it only meant that fear was still too deep in the recesses of their unadmitted minds. He knew they were afraid of the bullet and the blade, but more than those they were afraid of being afraid. If he had his way, he'd have them never admit to it. Neither admittance nor confession could lessen the feeling of its hold.

But Napoleon's mood was not their mood and it could never be because he rarely saw them as men anymore. He did not know when it first happened, but to him they were merely the beings that inhabited the human shapes they occupied. When they were killed, or their time was up, or they ran away, the shape similarly went away until it was filled again by another. Until that time it was vacant and remained so until it was filled by another being who stepped inside.

Then Extra Billy rode in. He wore a wide smile on his face,

as if instead of a hard ride he'd been lollygagging about, as if
all the time in the world was his own. Extra Billy had ridden
with him when they crossed the international line in March
and together they'd climbed the Barbicora Plateau in a cold
gale and almost froze to death, the snow so deep the horses
sank in the drifts and had to be dug out. They rode with blankets over their shoulders and they slept in the saddle holding the reins. They lived on Armour canned rations and had
to cut away the leather stirrup hoods to resole their boots.
When the horses lamed there was nothing they could do except remove the shoes and let them go. Icicles formed in their
beards, water froze in canteens, and each morning they awoke
covered with snow. When they ran out of food they shot a
whitetail and ate like wolves, sucking its blood from handfuls
of snow. The horses were so hungry they chewed their halter shanks. Extra Billy was a hard-boiled guy. He didn't care.
He'd piss in the wind.

Extra Billy's knife scar was crimsoned and it was as if another smile was decorating his grizzled face. He knew there
was no need to rush. He knew they'd entered into the design
of another.

He shook his head at the sight of the man and he began to
smile too. His smile grew wide and he could not stop shaking
his head—how fortunate he'd been to at least have drawn
this one.

"You enjoying yourself, Trooper?" Napoleon asked, as he
rolled a cigarette.

"Just peachy, sir."

"See anything out there you like?"

"Nothing much to speak of."

"Then what do you like?" He scraped a match off his thigh and struck fire. He held up the match and pulled deep on his cigarette.

"I was thinking about when we got back I'd like to drink my face off."

"It's been a while," he said as he watched the smoke that curled from his cigarette. "How long has it been?"

"It's been a long long while."

"Some days you just can't drink enough," he said.

They both knew the question of how much longer they could run would be answered that day and they would not be the ones doing the answering.

"Do you think it's time to order the coffins?" Napoleon said.

"Nossir, not yet."

Napoleon looked to the earth, the sky and the sun. He gazed into the nullity beyond.

8

BY LATE DAY the horses' backs were feverish under the saddles and the hard ride was swelling them. It would not be long before they would start breaking down and then they'd be afoot. But the horses had to last until they couldn't be spurred any further and then they'd make their stand. He began to search the landscape with that in mind, as escape now seemed remote and soon this pursuit would be forced to a conclusion.

He knew their pursuers had by now changed mounts at least once if not twice and rode fresh horses. The land was heated worse than he could remember and the sky was starting to twitch.

The same way wolves relay a deer, they were being cut off and worn down and shepherded further and further from their sanctuary. They should be steering north by northeast, but every time he made the move they were turned again.

Right now they could neither be taken nor could they escape the deadly game. He did not know how much longer they could last. Success in an attempt to pursue or retreat depended on the experience of the horses and their powers and the riders riding them, and that he knew was impossible. He did not want to fight with these men.

Cut off again, they retreated southward and when they came to the railroad tracks he faced about. He pulled up the Rattler horse and waited. Something had been decided. The distant riders understood the fatigue he and his horses were experiencing and were closing their stalking distance. Still, their horses seemed to gather heart and were ready to work. The Rattler jigged and bounced, scraping ties and kicking ballast and its shoes set sparks flying from the rails. Its neck rose up like a cock bird's and it pealed off a long series of high withering neighs. A sign from the Rattler horse, he thought, to halt their flight and engage, but not here, not yet. He knew you had to leave something inside a horse so it could help you when you needed it and the time of need was swiftly approaching. He would use up the horses, drawing their last full measure, and only then he would fight.

"He would challenge them," Stableforth said, admiring the Rattler horse.

"More like he'd fuck 'em," he said.

Stableforth repeated this as if a line heard at the theater. He thought it very funny and said so several times. The fool still did not understand the game that was afoot and however much he wanted him to understand, he knew the only lesson that would teach him and the price of that knowledge.

"Where are those wagons?" Bandy asked him as he rode in, but he did not reply because in Bandy's voice was the little boy and desperation. He needed Bandy to be a man. In all ways he needed every one of them to be better than they were and he needed to be better than himself.

"Keep your chin up," he told the boy. "Be steady."

A wind flared up and a dust devil scuttled across the land.

Then another. Behind them scattered rifle fire broke out. It was long range and ineffective, but the first time these green men had ever been fired on.

"Let's get moving," he said, his orders given to the horse, and there they would leave behind another fragment of their lives.

They crossed the railroad tracks, the horses' shoes clattering on the steel rails and shifting as much weight as possible onto his hindquarters, the Rattler horse plunged over the edge with fore hoofs in the air. It slid and broke a way down the steep, ballast-laden bank. They descended the other side in a small avalanche of stone and scree to the rocky soil below. The other horses sat to arrest their slides and at the bottom paused and found their strength in the crupper. Then they lifted up and scrambled onto their legs and were on the run again.

In the sky there was developing a violent light. If these men were horses, he thought. If only we were horses. There was a cloud bank to the east and a rolling squall line was coming out of the north and it was in this direction he turned and stretched out the Rattler.

To the west, brief clouds of dust were beginning to congregate and rise and still the high hot sun was beating on them, tolling them down. The distant riders continued to close and their envelopments continued to cut them off. They were fired upon, but the shots were mere sound and seemed without purpose except to usher them along. In all his soldiering he'd never seen such, or been so fooled. The trap was more elaborate than at first he realized and however he looked at

it, he was now convinced he'd been leading them to this encounter: since a day ago, since two days ago, even three, as he
bore them in the direction of the coming storm.

The sky to the west swirled with its rising dust and now
seemed strangely luminous. He pulled up and scanning
the countryside with the field glasses he searched the likely
draws for bushwhackers, for cover, for escape. Clear to see,
an enormous weather formation surrounded by copper light
was shaping up the valley and there was no way to tell which
direction it would blow. Dust motes were catching the distant
light and making watery shafts. The light was dense and yel-
lowing and seemed impenetrable. He could feel the Rattler's
sides ticking like a clock under his hand. Whatever was coming was coming fast and whatever it was, it was going to be
bad and if it was bad enough it could give them a slim kind of
chance and maybe even save them.

He reined up the Rattler and stood in the stirrups, the nick-
ering horse dancing beneath him and he waved them on.

Hurry, his mind kept whispering as the blood beat in his
temples. The horse was champing at the bit, scattering flecks
of foam, wanting the rein. A scribble of lightning etched the
sky, milliseconds of stroke, quarter seconds of flash. It was the
lightning that went before the storm and each added second
of time was filled with consequence. Death was on the flank
not a mile away and he was in the quest of lightning.

"What are you going to do?" Bandy said as he rode in. He
spoke as if the situation had little to do with him. But how
could he know, being so young and yet to experience an enemy that sincerely wanted to kill him.

"Something will come to mind," he reassured the boy.

"I guess this means we're going to miss the motion picture tonight," Bandy said.

"Yes, son. It looks that way." He smiled. He could not help himself for how boyish the observation and he thought perhaps something was inside the boy that would serve the troop and in turn deliver him.

When the others were near he put spurs to his horse, but the Rattler, so mettlesome and aroused, had already taken the rein it wanted.

By now the horses were rolling their bloodshot eyes and their sides were sunk in and they were gasping for breath, but still they were answering the call, still they were stretching their necks for power and distance, so afraid the Rattler would leave them behind.

He could hear a peculiar, long-drawn sighing that grew louder. A brief troughing wind sprang up and skifts of sand lifted and blew and died away. At first the sky was yellow with sunlight refracting in the particle dense air and yet it was remarkably windless after the first wind, as if the storm had collected all the wind in the land.

There was a deep hollow silence he remembered and an eerie green glow in the sky and then explosive thunders boomed and then they boomed again and did not stop, as if armies were fighting in the clouds, and then it burst upon them with thunderclaps of artillery, a nameless storm with inconceivable power.

At first it was rainless and began slowly to build a thundery dust cloud that seemed to extend for several miles and through this they were caught in the billowing and were soon choking on the gritted and sculling wind. The wind increased and the sand lifted higher and blew cursive serifs that wrapped their bodies and cut their faces. While at first the wind blew against them, now the wind blew through them. They wore their goggles to keep the stinging from their eyes and pulled neckerchiefs to keep their throats clear.

Inside the storm the world was shoreless and full of nothing. The air was rolling over at the same time it was plunging to earth and rooting up and lifting the loose debris. It was as if the darkness was rising from the depths of the earth and swallowing the mountains and the sky.

In the storm it seemed as if nothing was real or would ever be real again. There was no time except time immediate. There was no place. They were not where they were and there was no worse danger than they were experiencing. There was no earth and there was no sky. There was no direction; the compass needle, if he could have seen it, would have swirled in his hand. The storm was everything.

He kept them close together as best he could. It was fundamental. He could not allow them to become separated. The Rattler jerked its head and pricked its ears on high alert. The big stallion reared up to the vertical and settled as if floated to the ground on wings, its ears bent back and its mane hackled. The Rattler was telling him it wanted to run, it needed to run and to let the others follow if they could. He knew if they ran in the storm the Rattler could outrun the others and the horse would save him. In the storm he could disappear. He knew if he only had himself to save this he could do. He knew

Extra Billy would make it too. But the rest would become lost and picked off one by one like so many flowers in a bloody garden.

He let the Rattler horse have its head.

They rode hard. He touched his spurs to the Rattler horse and the horse lengthened stride and stretched it out and found even more speed. He knew he could outrun their pursuers before they could circle and close again. Time and again he'd known this. At the same time he knew his responsibility lay with his men.

Don't think that way, he thought. Service and duty, he thought.

He made the horse to slacken its speed.

Their pursuers became the filled-in outlines of men on horses and far off or close he could not tell in the airborne fields of lifted and sheeting earth whose side they were on. The dense veil of sand cut like a razor when it lashed against him. It was an ill wind lifting, dusting and setting grit to fly at ever increasing velocity. It lifted the Rattler's tail and mane and flattened them like blown over grass. There was a burning smell the wind carried and it filled his nostrils.

He pulled up and waited for the men to ride in. Their hats were torn from their heads and their buttons undone by the wind. Then Extra Billy rode in, ransacked and steadfast, bringing up the rear, ushering in the failing riders. One of his eyes was closed and other was weeping for the dust blown into it.

Napoleon was shamed to have run to save himself. He was shamed by this man's ignorant loyalty and the responsibility it conferred. He stepped the Rattler horse to his side as if to talk, but he simply wanted to be close to the man if only for a moment. As he came alongside Extra Billy's horse, its tail suddenly flickered and snapped and it happened again with a crackle and then the horse's mane began to light and dance in the air. A jagged spear of light connected them and they were stung and shocked by its viciousness.

He reached for the Springfield and when he touched the steel he was jolted again by another charge of static electricity. Their dull and lusterless metals began to glow with a bluish white light as if hot cadmium adorned them and in the exchange of current they were flush with radiance.

Blue sparks began coming off all their metals and stinging them in their hands and arms and causing their teeth to grind. The energy of static electricity made by the scraping motes of sand, unable to ground out, was crackling and hissing and discharging all about them into the dry air and they glowed, and as the others gathered around them, their fields connected and they were all for a time lit this way, blue and white and awed inside the storm.

9

HE CALLED FOR THEM to follow and made a nicking sound and the Rattler broke for full gallop, hocks beneath, forehand lightened and body extended. The surge was instant and if he'd not called it up himself it would have left him sitting in the dirt.

The horse seemed to turn of its own accord into the canyon wall and down a long stony corridor overhung with cliffs. It was a giant space they were entering, but he knew it was not as it appeared. He knew they were being directed and it was by intention they were riding into this place and any slim hope for escape in the storm was gone.

To his right was a first outcropping of rock and then there was one to the left and behind it were armed men. Then the right wall began to rise and even more abruptly the left wall shot up from the desert floor and the corridor began to narrow. The trail twisted and wound among the rocks with high rock walls necking and rising overhead and seemed a strange, critical entrance into another world. The shadows deepened and joined as they continued into the funnel's spout, the storm raging down its walls.

There would be no escape. They continued on into the canyon and the canyon walls closing on them, as if into an hourglass they were blown with the sand by the wind. He knew at the next turn or the next there would be no opening but a wall of stone, and no way out. He looked back with bewilderment into the storm of wind and sand. Where did it go wrong? What should he have seen that he did not see? He was angry with himself. Try as he might he could not have turned the advantage. If he'd attempted to break through they would have been shot to pieces. His only course was to hold off death as long as he could. He set his teeth.

By now there was not much left in man or horse. He'd held off as long as he could and he could not dwell on possibility any longer. It was time for the coming conclusions. Already the horses were tightening up, their loins and croups stiffening with agony after so extended and fast a trip they'd endured. Soon they would have difficulty moving and stop and collapse, or they would trip, or their legs would buckle and they'd go down, their eyes mystified by the dull hollows of pain.

Either wall would serve as a strong point, but the west wall would deepen first and shadow the longest. It was tumbled where boulders had fallen from its heights and strewn the desert floor. This was their best advantage. It was also their only one. He made his decision to anchor their thin line at the west wall and extend it out from there. They would hold this way as long as they could and then they would close on the strong point at the west wall and dig in.

Get closer to the ground, he told himself. Get under the storm.

He dismounted the Rattler horse while it was still moving and tried to gentle its shivering and trembling chest. Its hide was dark with sweat down to its flanks and withers, its mouth a torrent of white combings.

There was nothing left in any of the horses. They were blown and jaded and fogged from every ounce of flight wrung from within them. They'd gotten everything out of them they possibly could and truth be told they were broken and they would never be fit again. He commanded the Rattler horse to lie down at the center of his forming line and it did so promptly. The air began to crackle again and he saw a flicker and the flash of a spark and soon they were bathed in the glow of long blue lights again. Then his troopers emerged from a cloud bank of dust, riding knee to knee, and were so close he could hear the drumming of the horses' lungs and they too were similarly lit in blue, their bodies made luminous and for the briefest moment they were as if firedrakes.

As the rest staggered in, one after another, rearing and plunging, trails of dust and sand devils catching up with them, he directed them into position. He did not give their green minds an inch of leeway. In one hand he held the Springfield and in the other he held bandoleers of clipped ammunition.

"Get them down," he yelled. "Get them down," and when Turner's horse would not go down where he directed it, he stepped forward, unholstered his .45, and shot it through the ear.

"You killed him," Turner said, his horrified words torn off in the ferocious wind.

"We kilt these horses two hours ago," he said.

His blood was blunt and his voice clear and cold. He commanded Extra Billy to his right and to his left he placed

Preston, Stableforth, and Turner in order. He posted Bandy at the wall by a steep declivity with sheltering rocks a short climb away.

There came a great cracking sound, as if a rifle discharged, and a horse screamed. He whirled on the sound, the Springfield at his shoulder. The gray Preston rode had broken a leg where it stood and fallen to the hard ground. Jagged white bone tore through the animal's shoulder and stabbed out at the light. Without hesitating, he drew the muzzle of the .45 to the horse's ear and ended its life.

"We have some work to do today," he told them, as if what just happened hadn't happened at all. "It will require some courage."

He felt the heat flow emanating from his belly and a blood thrill traveling his arteries and returning veins. He called down his darker nature and was contemptuous of the awes and terrors of his history.

Then he told them, "I wouldn't have no other company for it, not for all the tea in China," and their spirits soared and they smiled and laughed for how businesslike he'd suddenly become and how much in that moment they loved him and feared him. His eyes caught the look and the smile on the boy's face, the haunt in his eyes. He turned to Preston and looked into him. By Preston's own account he'd already killed about one of everything that crawled, walked, slithered, flew, or swam. Except a man. He'd hunted, but he'd never hunted a man or been hunted by one. He knew he was anxious for his chance at distinction. Now it just might come.

On the ground at his feet the Rattler horse blew big sighs,

making the creak of leather. He reached down with his knife blade and cut the horse's bellyband and it sighed again with the release and stretched and pawed in the dirt. He kneeled down and touched the horse's shoulder. It was fine and flat and in the Rattler's eye he could see it knew his touch. This horse's bones, tendons, blood, muscles, and nervous substance had given him all it had that day and now it lay in the dry crackling dust in blue flame ready to stop bullets for him.

He opened his tobacco pouch and took a mouthful. His life seemed strange and silent and deathlike to him. He experienced a certain looseness in mind and thought. His earliest memories were of riding in the saddle in front of his mother. His grandfather had fought in old Mexico with Thomas Jackson and so too his father and now it would kill him and these men with him and this fine horse that lay at his feet.

He thought, It will require courage to die, and launched a brown smear of tobacco juice into the sand in response to his own thinking.

After the storm came a deep suspended silence and the dust it raised softened the horizon.

The day's protracted light was diminishing. The east wall painted red and gold and the west wall deepened in shadow. Present time was fading. Soon it would be dark and darkness would favor them. This day's distance did not amount to much in actual miles, but they'd been turned so many times he'd lost track of their immediate location. He wondered if there was a possible conclusion without consequence, a conclusion without truth or meaning. He didn't try to answer his wondering questions.

The weaving channels of dust blew away, the light wavered and behind it, somewhere, the orient sun was a ball of fire burning out the western sky and in the distance before him there were riders and they were coming out of that slant sunlight.

10

H E TOOK THEM to be a stray band of Villistas, soldaderas, broken and maimed Dorados, the shock cavalry who charged willingly and with such elan at the battles of Celaya and Agua Prieta and were mowed down by the Maxims and thrown onto the barbed-wire entanglements where they experienced slow and potting deaths.

Of the men and women, the women were always the hardest of the band. They knew what the men knew but they also knew what the men would never know. They knew hard work and hunger, but they also knew childbirth and they knew the death of those children. They knew rape and the death of their men. They knew hatred and no one returns hate like a woman.

They were armed with a variety of Winchester and Remington carbines and rifles and some carried Mausers and all manner of bladed weapons: knives, swords, and machetes. If indeed they were Dorados, they would attack. They always attacked.

Napoleon was kneeled and readied, awaiting the furious onslaught. But then he stood and faced his men. He stood straight as a ramrod, the stock of the Springfield tucked to his right side and the weight of it riding in the crook of his arm.

The new men had not had the occasion to see him in battle and they were braced by what they saw.

"Gentlemen," he said, turning to face them. "We have discovered the enemy," and at this they laughed.

He wasn't scared. It wasn't that he was brave or smart or stupid; it was just it wasn't worth a damn to be scared. Being scared killed you again and again before you died from what finally killed you. At least that's what the poets and the old heads had to say on the subject. He lifted the field glasses. He recognized one of the men as the horse trader who was speaking to his brother that morning.

"What is your thinking?" Stableforth called out.

"I think pr'aps it could be time for us to die." At this they laughed again.

"Right now?" Stableforth asked.

"Pretty near," he said. Having been outwitted and outflanked he understood how consequential his mistakes.

"Can we not do anything about it?"

"It's too late."

"Why?"

"It just is. If they pass against us, we lose," and this time, if they thought him funny, they did not laugh.

"It looks like we have gone and gotten ourselves into a pickle," Extra Billy chuckled.

He turned away from his men to face their pursuers. He lifted the field glasses and studied them again as he awaited their onslaught. He found the one woman and far distant he found the other. But they did not attack. They gathered within gunshot range and seemed to be deciding what to do. Although they had the overwhelming advantage, he trusted they knew they would pay a fearful toll in uprooting their fixed position.

"Now what's entered your mind?" Stableforth called out.

The trouble right now, he thought, is that there is no trouble.

Napoleon watched them intently as they held their council. He could not divine what their game was. They fought or they did not fight. It was not like them to play around this way. Patience in battle was not one of their traits and the reason their ranks were so winnowed. They struck and they struck hard. He stepped out in front of his thin line of men and then raised a hand and stopped. He waited and they made the sign that they would talk.

Three riders came forward and he walked out to meet them. One of them, the horse trader, stopped and then it was two that came forward, a man and a boy. The man wore the gold insignia of the Dorados. He was an old man and wore an eye patch and silver conchas adorned his belt. There were so few of these men left in their ragged uniforms, their dirty Stetsons, their ranks broken and diminished by their audacious method of battle.

The boy was an American. He wore leather cuffs and batwing chaps buckled up the backs of his legs. He wore a vest and beneath his vest he wore an orchid-colored shirt with a placard front. A silk bandanna was knotted at his neck. Napoelon figured him a swamper on some remote and desolate ranch living alone in a line shack and fed up with the life and come south to seek his fortune. The boy had sharp clean features and maybe at one time a sweetness of nature, but in his face his eyes were those of a schemer and this he could not mask.

"I would speak a word with you," the boy said.

"How's wages?"

The boy leveled on him with a flat stare. His cheeks and lips reddened and his head suddenly seemed uncomfortable on his neck. The boy wasn't much older than Bandy, but already he was ruined.

"I know my price," the boy said.

"It's some bloody business you've taken up," Napoleon said, but he felt no particular hatred for the boy.

"That ain't none of your business," the boy said.

"I was just asking."

"I follow myself," the boy said.

The man said something to Napoleon and made a gesture, pointed to the .45 he wore in his shoulder rig. Napoleon knew some words in their language but he would not speak them. The man was interested in how the harness was strung that carried his holster. He then unholstered his own .45 and held it out. Its grips were inlaid with mother-of-pearl. He wanted Napoleon to take it in his hands and hold it and admire it.

"Very nice," he said, nodding his head, and the man nodded his head, pleased with their agreeing. Napoleon admired the inlay and sighted down the barrel. Then he returned it to the man who was still nodding.

"It ain't what you think with me," the boy said.

"I have eyes to see."

"Maybe you ain't seen what I seen."

"Maybe I ain't," he said. "Maybe I seen worse."

"If you're waiting for me to fall down on my knees and beg your forgiveness, it ain't going to happen. I ain't going to beg you. There's nothing you have that I want from you."

"I don't want anybody begging."

"That's good because I have begged all my life. Begged men and begged God and begged the land."

"Who are they?"

The boy looked back over his shoulder at those he represented and then back at him.

"They are their own selves," he said.

"What do they want?"

"They want him, the tall one," the boy said, pointing with his slow unmoving finger at the position in their line held by Preston.

"Him? What do they want him for?"

"I don't know."

"Ransom?"

"That's what I'd do."

"I can't see myself doing that."

"I already told them you wouldn't."

"Tell them I ain't giving up nobody to them."

"Like I said. I already told them."

"Then tell them again," he said, and turned and walked away from them.

He had little doubt the boy was capable of shooting him in the back, but he did not think he would do so. The boy answered to others and he took him to be realizing he'd gotten in over his head when he signed on with the company he traveled in. His life would be a short one.

"What do they want?" Stableforth asked.

"Surrender," he barked.

"What are we going to do?"

"Not surrender," he said with all serenity.

He did not know if it were now to die, but like the ancient Greeks they would man their small citadel of wind-guttered rocks and congregated sands. They would stand and hold to the end. There was no alternative.

He went to the wall where Bandy was positioned in the rocks. The boy's eyes were enormous and filled with ghosts. He was gripping his collar and his thumb was in his mouth. A band of white freckled skin showed at his throat.

Napoleon thought to explain their situation but knew how long the explanation would have to be before the boy understood. It needed to be understood by instinct and even with time he knew the boy was incapable of acquiring all that was necessary. He knew how grave and that was enough. Whether or not he'd do as he was told, that was another matter. He took the boy's rifle as if to inspect it.

"Have you quit yourself?" he asked him so only he could hear.

"I'm praying."

"What are you praying for, or can't you tell me?" He spoke softly to the boy lest he should come unstrung and fly away in pieces.

"Prayers ain't wishes," Bandy said, and began to hiccup.

"Then you can tell me?"

"Peace and quiet," Bandy said, trying to arrest the spasms. "I'm praying for peace and quiet."

"I sometimes wonder if heaven is open to our kind. Do you have any thoughts on that you'd want to share?"

"They'll take you," he said. "They take everyone."

"They don't sound too particular," he said. "I don't know if I'd want to be in such company as that."

To this, Bandy's face colored and he smiled, an emotion suspended in time and then he asked, "What's going to happen?"

"I think things could get bad very soon," he told him.

"What are they going to do?"

"Well, there's going to be some noise real quick and then we are going to be in trouble."

He held the boy's attention with gentle eyes the boy had not seen before. He spoke quietly, softly, adamantly. In almost a whisper he told him if he saw an opportunity he was to go up that wall and over the top without being seen. He was to run some but not far and then he was to burrow down inside the earth and rock and hide until the stars came out and even then he was to wait a good long time. From his trouser pocket he removed the compass and handed it to the boy. He told him to follow the needle north by northeast.

"Don't look up," he said sharply. He did not want anyone to see him do that and draw conclusions. "It ain't easy, but I have already looked up there and I know it can be done. I know you can do it."

"What about you?"

"If I am not back before you then you will come look for me."

"Yessir."

"Don't let me down."

"Nossir," the boy said, and with his swollen mouth he made a crooked grin.

Then he returned to the boy his rifle. The boy nodded and Napoleon let him back into the rocks where they would all close after the first skirmish.

"Don't kill no one yet," Napoleon told them when he returned from the wall.

"I will if I can," Turner said.

"No you won't," he said. "You will god damn kill when I tell you to god damn kill and not before."

Then they waited.

His concern was not that these men would shoot, but that they wouldn't shoot when the time came. Getting a man to shoot another man, however much he was threatened, was not a thing you took for granted. If men could kill with their mouths, there would be a lot of dead, but when it came to pulling the trigger on another man, Napoleon had seen men stare in awe as they were run over and slaughtered.

He kneeled on one knee in the sand, the Springfield resting in the cradle of his arms. He could hear the separable sounds of their gathering in the silence. The deal was he could give up one man and save four. Given the circumstances, it was a good deal. But how could he trust the deal and if the deal was trustworthy, who would ever trust to ride with him again?

Eventually we all die, Napoleon thought. Sooner or later, what does it matter? The moment of death is not important. He wiped his mouth with the back of his hand. He told them there'd be a show, there was always a show, and to keep their heads down. At that correct moment a confirming bullet cut the air above him and then he heard the all but silent report of the distant gun. From long distance, a desultory fire began. He knew if they wanted him dead they would have shot him by now.

The Rattler horse raised its head and eyed him. It sneezed, convulsing its body and then it lay back down and blew a gust of breath scattering the sand and grit at its nostrils.

Another bullet passed him by. There is a sound a bullet makes when it cuts through the air. It's a zip that sings and whoops and each is different. That one was a Spitzer, a round fired from a Mauser. Napoleon knew because he had heard them before. To hear them you have to be very close. Having been that close, close enough to hear, he never forgot what he'd heard.

"Those bastards," Turner said.

"Keep your god damn heads down or you'll stop one for sure."

"But the bastards are shooting at us."

"You are not being shot at personally," he told the man. He could not remember when he stopped hating those who were trying to kill him. After all, he was trying to kill them too. He'd abandoned hatred somewhere on the plains of Montana or the jungles of the Philippines. He wasn't sure, but no matter, it wasn't good to hate. It always seemed to get in the way of doing the job, always seemed to take more than it ever gave back, always seemed to get the hater killed sooner than he otherwise might have been killed.

Time passed with sporadic and errant fire but without any sign of them. He cast an expectant look in their direction and as if called forth they suddenly appeared. Riders shook out and began working their way in. They paused to fire and then moved closer. They were not in a killing mood. There was something they wanted and would rather not die in getting it. He set his jaw and held his position. Keep a good heart, he told himself, an eye full of light. Show no fear. Be free of dangerous passion. Let nothing confuse the natural instinct toward violence.

The skirmishers moved closer, a Dorado on a magnificent white horse out in front. He wore pistols at his waist and rode in a graceful position, as if standing upright in his seat. The hilt of a saber showed from a scabbard on the right of his saddle. He wore cartridge belts strapped across his chest. That he was holding himself and his horse in reserve was clear to see. The horse was uncommon and he could not help but admire it, the arched neck, the swing of the back, the flexion and extension of the hindquarters. The horse moved as if touching the earth was not necessary, but pleasure and whimsy, as it danced from one diagonal to the other.

Kill the brave one, he thought, and let the others go home. The mere presence of his death in the ranks would sew discontent and they would learn fear.

The men who rode with the Dorado spread out to fill the canyon ground but followed close behind. Their horses were compact, not tall and leggy like his but full form and set low on their legs. Their pace was that of a forced walk. The men shot across their horses' necks but placed their shots so as not to kill. They plowed the earth and chipped stone and flattened their lead against rocks and ledges. The bullets hissed by like spit into a fire, and still he did not move his exposed position.

Then the Dorado fell forward onto the neck of his white

horse, shot through the heart, the blood pouring from his wound. Then came instant the flat cracking report of a rifle that was not a Springfield or Winchester or Mauser. It was Preston's custom-made English rifle and he was standing upright and still holding the butt tight to his shoulder, his cheek pressed to the wood.

For some reason the animal did not break but stopped and would not move and stood stock still on the center ground. Runnels of blood seeped from beneath the man and down the horse's shoulders. The heart pumped steadily, emptying the man's blood onto the horse's shoulders and legs until its white hide was caped red. The horse pawed and shrugged and the man slid to the ground, slowly at first and then all in a rush as if desperate to meet the rising earth and the forever that was waiting for him.

11

THE SOUND OF the shot echoed in the hollow air, seeming time without end, rebellowing off the rocky walls, and when finally diminished it was a sound like the sift and drag of sand. Men on both sides paused and were shocked at its event.

"You witless bastard," Napoleon said. "You have just kilt us."

But Preston seemed indifferent. He'd wanted to demonstrate his courage and this he would do, no matter how thoughtless, uncharitable, and condemning. What he would have and what was required made no difference to him.

"Don't fly at me," Preston said. "It's done and there's no undoing it."

"No. I'd say you are right on that account. There is no undoing it."

In the old days he'd have shot Preston on the spot for such insubordination and not even have been questioned. You only led by the consent of those you would lead. You only commanded because there were those who agreed to be commanded and he knew Preston was his failure. Napoleon wondered about himself. In how many battles had he fought on the side of murderers? How many times in his life would he have willingly changed sides?

With the death of the Dorado was the death of possibility. Now it was time come for them to encounter their fears. They would have to reach down and fetch up what was inside them, knowing they would surely die and there would be little time to spend hoping for deliverance and the wondering was it a Godless world.

His mind was quickened and was without doubt. Fire would now answer fire. There was no reality beyond this reality and all time was now. His green men would have their baptism in the desert. He knew Extra Billy had the murderous spirit, but would the rest of them? Being a long-range killer was one thing, but this would soon be a different matter. The lowness of their professional competence he'd experienced before. But this day they'd drop their blood because of it and if they knew anything they knew this.

With the westering sun the shadows lengthened and deepened. Overhead the sky was still light, but where they held was darkening. He recalled words his father read to him when he was a boy: *Stiffen the sinews, summon up the blood, . . . lend the eye a terrible aspect; . . . set the teeth and stretch the nostril wide, hold hard the breath and bend up every spirit.*

Suddenly the air sang and the rocks and ground stitched as if an iron needle driven by a great treadle and then was sound—the clatter of a machine gun. The bullets flashed overhead and ripped against the canyon walls and a thousand shards of stone flew in the air.

He threw the binoculars to Stableforth and instructed him to find the gunner and to do it now. The machine gun continued its clattering, lurching, stuttering, coughing, and the bullets continued to fly in all directions. The gunner had no apparent experience as the first bullets went into the ground and then climbed and swung wildly left and right and shot their holes in the sky.

He lay prone and perched on his elbows he wove his left arm through the sling of the Springfield. With Stableforth's directions he found the gunner in the crosshairs. The man was squatting and bouncing behind the weapon that controlled him. He timed the shot to the beating of his heart, squeezed the trigger ever so gently and absorbed the kick.

"You got him," Stableforth yelled out.

"That will teach them," Turner cried out.

"What are they doing now?" he said, resting his cheek on his bunched fist.

"Just looking at him."

"Is there another?"

"There doesn't seem to be."

"Then there won't be," he said, and then thought, Now they need a machine gunner.

Again, he measured their chances of life. It did not look good for the future but right now they were still alive. But now there were two dead and this would be unacceptable to them.

He stood and addressed his men.

"We are now the dead," he said, his voice as hard as death itself, "so fight like you cannot be kilt."

He puffed out his chest and strutted across the front of their line. He carried the Springfield, the butt tucked into the pit of his arm.

"They will come on us in a rush," he said, his left arm sweeping out before him.

He knew them well, their love of the shock tactic, the headlong charge a mile over rough ground, then eight hundred yards at full gallop, firing carbines and pistols. In the past the Dorados had paid dearly the fearful toll of attacking entrenched positions protected by concentric circles of coiled barbed wire. They jumped it and tangled in it, the wire barbs catching and hissing across the earth as it rose up to embrace what it'd caught in its snarling trap. Held in momentary arrest, the machine guns short hammer, and their bodies dying as threaded statues, upright and floating on wire spools as if sculpted for memorial.

As with the ancient Macedonians, the Dorados preferred the moral superiority of close combat over fighting at a distance and it got them killed. It was this moral superiority that so badly winnowed their numbers when again and again, they charged and were entangled in barbed wire and cut down in swaths by Maxims. That's how they'd come when they came. They didn't know any other way.

"Each man, do your best," was the rest of the more he could say.

Soon all hell would break loose and this would be a no-good place. The next actions would be motion undefined. Action requiring response. Action lurching off in directions beyond prediction. Knowing when to act yourself. And even then the odds unknown and changing so suddenly it would take a thousand patterns reconfiguring in an instant and an instant and an instant.

"Come on," he said, and as if summoned, mounted men pranced into view. He felt the judder in his stomach and snugged the Springfield to his ribs. What a story he would have to tell his brother when next he saw him.

"Ask and ye shall receive," he said, and stepped forward. He could feel the pounding of his arteries as they came on at a controlled pace and then broke into an all-out gallop, their ranks serried in their race to the enemy. They rode with reins in hand or reins in teeth and a pistol in each hand.

As they came on, his wildness flared inside him and the certitude that he should exist and his existence would not be taken away from him. The violence was not exciting to him but simple in calculation and fascinating in experience, and he knew he was ready and would soon enough experience the relief of conflict. He looked to the sky, the paired and silver sun dogs residing there, an omen of the forthcoming. He stepped again, stepped out to meet them. He thought, I am the first and the last and the always and raised the Springfield to his shoulder and emptied the clip. At first he could hear the rattle of the rifle bolt as three riders fell backward over their horses' croups and two more slumped forward onto their horses' necks as if a spell had been cast. Then he could only hear the fugue of repeated and interlocking explosions as he reloaded the Springfield and fired five more times and four riders fell headlong with stunning violence and a horse buckled and rushed down to the earth.

He loaded again and five more of the surging buckled and crashed down into the onrushing earth.

He watched as one of the fallen, his foot caught in the stirrup, pulled his pistol from off his hip and calmly shot down his own horse that was dragging him. He thought, What a remarkable feat and was proud of the man.

Still the charge came on as if forever, each horse animating the one next to it, and soon it was a race to his thin line, unrestrained and out of control, and they were crashing into his thin line. With a fury swifter than thought they sifted through them, threw their bodies back, collected their horses, wheeled, and came again, at top speed.

Turner was the first of their number to be shot and killed. The bullet went singing through his jaw and then he was shot again while stumbling forward, the second bullet nicking his heart through the hollow under his left shoulder. He held on in pain and amazement as the blood pumped from the hole in his ribs and washed his side.

"Get up," Napoleon yelled.

"I can't," Turner cried, his complexion whitening, his thready voice, little by little, the last of him.

"You have to," he yelled.

Another wave sifted through them as if a wind and there was the smoke of discharged powder. A rider carried a double-barreled hammer gun with pistol grips and sawed off to a short handy length. When he laid it down and fired there was a short stabbing flame of gunfire and it took Turner square in the face and he was gone.

Napoleon turned on the rider, his body corkscrewed, and pulled the trigger on the Springfield. The bullet found the back of the rider's skull and came out through the orbit of his eye. The man fell tangled in his stirrup and his crazed horse dragged him from the battlefield.

Preston and Stableforth were reloading. Extra Billy, the sleeves of his shirt rolled to his elbows, was stretching his palm flat trying to make it work. He'd been shot through the hand.

He looked up and glimpsed for Bandy in the rocks. He reloaded the Springfield. All around them were the fallen, the dead and mortally wounded, contorted and silent. All around them the crazed riderless horses, the chaos of stirrups and shod hooves bludgeoning the air and then they were gone.

The blood pounding in his arteries, he went down on one knee and whistling through his teeth, he stroked the cheek of the Rattler horse. The horse flashed a clean dark eye on him and held his gaze. Softly whistling he covered its eye with his hand. The horse laid back its ears and he felt the lid blink and close. They breathed together for a few moments and then he stood erect and struck a match and made a show of lighting a cigarette. He knew they'd come again.

This time there came a lone rider, a Yaqui, who rode a white horse naked with a bloody knife clenched in his teeth. The white horse's small hooves barely touching the ground, it crossed in snorts and huffs from deep in its chest. They watched it come on, red nostriled, its eyes rolling back, its entire body quivering with wildness in its desperate run.

The Yaqui, smeared with the sweat and foam and blood, rode without saddle or bridle and did not turn off but came straight for them, the white horse red and wet and mesmerizing and instantly was rearing in their midst and so near he could see its eyes and he swore it was an albino. The Yaqui, swart and hard faced and eyes black as wells, had cut incisions in the hide of the white horse, releasing the bright hot arterial blood contained within, and now it coursed the horse's sides. The white horse reared and plunged, but the rider kept his seat. The white horse reared upward in pirouette, its eyes wide and fear bright, its front hooves pawing the air as rivulets of blood spun from its turning body, spun in the air, spun in their eyes. The blood sprayed from its shoulders and fore-arms, its croup and stifle. The air was flung with the white horse's blood as red as scarlet as the horse whirled about and they fought back, bewildered by what horror was unleashed in their center. The Yaqui came straight at him and when he held his ground whooped and flared off to the side and then came again.

He leveled the Springfield to fire from his hip, but it was Extra Billy, his hand bullet mangled, who raised his .45 and shot the white horse in the head two times before it fell. The horse rushed down to the earth, the quivering animal at his feet, and when it fell he stepped forward and shot the naked tumbling rider in the back and chest and in the back again, ejected the empty magazine, and slammed home another.

Extra Billy looked up, and across the distance they found each other's eyes. His skin was burnished amber with sun. His eyes alight, he held up his bloody hand, his fingers curved as if holding a whisky glass. He held his hand up too and when Extra Billy tilted his empty hand to his lips, he nodded and drank with him from the curl of his fingers.

Then they were coming again and from above it must have appeared as a violent storm. Their world was bounded by the loom work of rock, steel, lead, and fire. There was sluicing blood, torn flesh, split bones, and concurrent explosions.

He fired into a ewe-necked mare as it barreled in his direction, intent on barging him to the ground and running him beneath its hooves. He stepped aside at the last moment as it made its pass but was so close the rider slashed with his whip and kicked out and caught Napoleon with a vicious kick in the chest. Staggering and quivering, he fell back, desperate to shake off the thundering shock of the blow. He could not find his breath and could not keep his feet.

The fight became desperate at every elevation: men on knees and men standing, men on horseback and men falling from horseback and still fighting, still shooting, still cutting the air with bullet lead and steel blades as their bodies curved and unfolded and knifed to the hard stony ground.

Another gun exploded off his right ear and he was deafened. He fired the .45 into the massed riders and the heavy bullets knocked men against men, made horses scream. He emptied the clip and drove in another. They could count life in the chaos of brass shell casings that littered the ground. They could count life in the slashed and exploding air. They could count life in the fallen warhorses, the stained and torn and moiled earth.

"Please help me," cried a voice winnowed in the throat. He heard the cry, the voice a crying airless falsetto filled with a childlike fear. "Please help me."

It was Stableforth. A bullet had cut his throat and he could barely speak. He held his hand clasped to his neck and still his blood leaked from between his fingers. A second bullet shot him through his belly and he buckled forward holding his ripped guts as if swung on a hinged prong. He was making an unearthly moaning sound, his body folded in half. The bullet had passed through his bowels and destroyed them and he must have thought a bonfire lit inside his belly.

He knew they must see their commander and so he stood in the midst of their onslaught and as they came again in another wave he emptied the clip of his .45 into them and slammed home yet another. At his feet fell more of the horses and riders.

He looked again to Stableforth. Wide eyed and helpless looking, he sat holding his own entrails — yellow, purple and gray — in the dimming light. He was dying in his passage from one convulsion and into another. He must have known there would be no deliverance from death because all at once he lifted his .45, put the barrel in his mouth, and pulled the trigger.

Napoleon snapped cold with ferocity. It was a profound logic that ruled the chaos. He looked up and the dark front of the sky was full of fiery shapes and darting black figures. Another rider came at him and he could hear him by the horse he rode, a roaring broken-winded horse. He turned and the horse was crashing against his chest before he could move. The blow from the horse knocked the air from inside his chest and he was spun around and knocked back. His feet left the ground and he was hurtling for the short distance it took to meet the rushing ground.

His .45 lost, he raised himself onto his knees and turned on his waist to see the flash of a machete above his head. It paused as if the tipped wing of a steel bird about to plunge. His killer had a gold tooth and a black mustache and wore white trousers patched at the knees. He could see the whites of his eyes and his white teeth. His eyes were black and his face, the view of his mind, was as if a face in rictus.

His guts twisted. He knew he was dead and was wondering what death would be like when the Rattler horse, lithe as a cat, lurched onto its front feet, stretched out with its long neck and head and took the man's whole face in its wide mouth. The bite swallowed whatever cry there might have been. It tore away the man's nose and cheek meat, his lips and mustache and his eyebrows and all the skin and meat that was the man's face.

The place where the man's face had been was turned to blood. He stood horribly crimsoned with the hot blood springing from his faceless head and wreathing his neck and caping his shoulders. Then came his sourceless scream. It pitched and seized and pitched again. It stayed in the air even as he collapsed to the ground where he quivered and trembled, wanting to touch his face but unable to.

Napoleon called out and turned as Extra Billy, already aware, had made his own turn on the machete and was swung through and aligning his aim for the shot when he was struck by a deadly bullet gliding into his side and it cut him down. The bullet that found his chest hurled him sideways and crumpled him to the ground where he lay in the shakes of death.

He knew that feeling. He had been shot before, his insides flashing as if suddenly a pool of hell.

Extra Billy opened his mouth to groan but was soundless for how consuming the quenchless fire that'd been lit in the mangling of his chest. Already his clothes were soggy with blood as it pumped from inside him with each convulsive twitch. Blood crept from the corner of his mouth and down his chin. Extra Billy was a hard one and the hard ones don't let go easily. He listened to the terrible gasping of the man's last moments, the tiniest gusts of air leaving his lungs. He was dying by seconds and in agony as his heart pumped his blood from his body onto the floor of the earth. Then he raised an arm as if reaching for the distance and when his arm fell he was gone. Extra Billy had been a good man and he wished for him some swifter means of death, but that was not the one given him.

Napoleon turned again, searching the ground for a weapon. The place he stood had become a lake of blood and was as if every death and misery in human experience was concentrated at his feet. He caught sight of Preston standing erect amid the ruck of battle. He was holding up his hand and looking at it in amazement. His index finger had been shot away at the second joint. He was then laying down his rifle and holding his arms wide open as if in supplication.

Their small world was a blur of sound and light and the blood still blooming from the many wounds. He cast a desperate glance to the rock wall where Bandy was stationed. He hoped to see the boy scurrying the heights, the last of his legs disappearing over the top, but there was no sign of the boy he could find.

He turned again and to his amazement, Extra Billy was staggering beside him, as if half awake, half asleep. His cold eyes were smiling, his skin burnished amber and in his bloody hand he held a .45. Standing his legs astraddle he shot down three men before the guns turned on him again. The bullets shattered through his laddered ribs, lacerated his heart, and delivered unto him the hardest truth.

Then a brilliant light exploded in his own head and was a suffusion of blunt and liquid pain. He fought against the sensation that was sweeping through him. He cried out his brother's name, but he could not endure the red-violet explosion inside his head and the light eclipsed and this day's work was over for him as well and that was the last he knew of the battle.

12

TWO RIDERS CAME FORWARD. They sat above him on horseback, their horses' tails whisking flies. They carried Mausers and sheathed machetes down their backs, the hilts in reach at their shoulders. One man's britches were torn away at the knees and the other wore canvas leggings from another war in a previous century.

For all the pain he felt, in his head and body were the promises of pain yet to be experienced as all around him lay the glassy-eyed dead. When he stood, the last of that scene came to him in the faint groans of one of the fallen. It did not matter who it was, one of his or one of theirs, the man's groans struck upon his heart as a hammer might. So were the last of the screams and sighs and tears and groans of that small place where men fought and died so fiercely. Never again would they rise up from the ground. Never again would they fight on this given earth.

He wanted to look to the wall. Had the boy been able to climb the wall or crawl inside the rock itself and squirrel himself away? He'd experienced enough such miracles to accept the miraculous as common enough. He hoped the boy was so favored this day.

Then he watched as Preston stood up from the ground. His head had been cut by blade or bullet and the opening bled in a curtain down the side of his face. He moved a hand as if waving off a fly, searching the air for his shot-away finger. He held his pistol in his other hand and then he let it slip from his hand.

The two riders indicated they were to take off their boots and hand them up. They tossed out gunnysacks and gestured they were to be placed over their heads. Then they flung out the long loops of their reatas and caught them in their nooses and pulled tight. The braided rawhide was smooth and light but closed tight as a vice at their necks. The riders dallied the ropes around their saddle horns as they directed the turning of their horses and slowly Napoleon and Preston were led away.

As they stumbled along they could hear as they were joined by more riders in ever-increasing numbers. They were jostled and bumped and fell down more than once, struggling blindly to regain their footing lest they be strangled to death because the riders did not stop. They continued on, the horses' walk slow and inexorable and fixed in direction.

Forced to go bootless it wasn't long before Napoleon had very little skin left on the soles of his feet. The land pricked and slivered, spiked and burned, and his feet stung and were as if set afire and the airless and heated gunnysack was soon a suffocating ordeal.

"Steady," he kept saying. His head throbbed and he staggered like a drunken man. "Steady. Keep your legs."

He then fell and hit his head and was dragged by his neck

because he was unconscious for a time. When he came to, he realized some last and desperate effort to live had twisted his right arm in the rawhide and held on; otherwise he would have been strangled because they did not stop for him and kept going. He was being dragged by the rope over the rocks and through the briary mesquite. Then mercifully, the rider paused to light a cigarette and he was able to gain his feet again.

After a long hard walk they were prodded onto horseback and with riders to the right and left of them they rode hard from the scene of the battle. How far they rode or in what direction he could not keep his calculation. His lungs ached for breath and agonizing pain stabbed at his temples and the fire in his feet burned into his legs. The land sloped gently upward and he knew they were climbing, but that was all. They could be climbing anywhere, in any direction. The trail leveled for a time and then became steeper yet. His mind's exertion was fully directed at not passing out and falling from the horse, because to have fallen from the horse without sight, there would be no way to turn, to reach, to catch the ground, to not land on his head and break his neck. So he clung to the saddle horn and a fistful of mane and reasoned if he fell he'd hold to these, even if his arms were to break.

Then, after what seemed forever, they were stopped and dismounted. He stepped gingerly because he could not now feel his feet and his legs were simply the posts his body was perched upon. When the gunnysack was lifted from his head the first light he saw was the fading light of dusk, the dark light before darkness, the light before the silver shine of the stars. He became aware of a ringing in his ears, but then it stopped.

Then there was another sound and at first he could not figure out what it was and then he understood it to be a baby crying. Then there was the clinking of bridles and a mule brayed and then all sound rushed in and he could hear again.

They were in some mountain notch, the place of a secluded encampment with no sign of a way in or out. There was water and grass and growing on the periphery were stunted pine and live oak.

There were several dozen of them and they were a motley band of soldiers, women and children. They were all ages and their features ranged from brown-skinned Indian to blue-eyed Spanish. Some few rode richly furnished mounts while for others a sheepskin tied to the horse's back was enough.

The women were preparing the evening meal. They wore green and blue dresses with red sashes tied about their waists and shawls they wore over their shoulders and sometimes their heads. They were unloading mules that were packed with firewood, kettles and sacks of beans and corn and braided chilies.

These women, he wondered, how many of their sons, brothers, lovers, husbands had he killed this day?

Soon there were fires burning and they hung cuts of meat from the newly slaughtered beeves on iron spits where the slabs of beef smoked and roasted. A large copper boiler shined in the firelight. In that they'd make their frijoles. The corn they ground by hand they mixed with lard. Soon there were yellow stacks of tortillas piling up beside the hot kettles. There would be beef, frijoles and parched corn, and tortillas baked on fires in ovens fashioned from oil cans.

There were some riders who never dismounted and had their tortillas and frijoles and beef handed up to them. These were the Dorados—the chosen men who died so willingly, and this evening there were some fewer than who started the day. He admired them as warriors. They were rare to surrender and as impractical as it might seem, they were willing to die for their honor.

The grueling ride had been difficult for Preston. He was much weakened and near to shattered. With his first step he collapsed on the ground where he still lay. He appeared obsessed with his missing finger as he could not seem to avert his eyes. He cradled that hand in his other as if a small wounded other.

Napoleon thought to say something to Preston as he was his commander and they were comrades and fellow countrymen, but he could not help the anger he felt. So it was Preston who spoke first.

"We are in a suffering condition," he said, clasping his wounded, blood-caked hand to his chest.

"Stop sniveling," Napoleon said. "You will shame them." He carefully let himself to the ground close to Preston.

"What do they want?"

"We will find out what they want when they want us to know."

From where he lay he watched men pitching shovels into the dry dusty earth. He at first thought they were digging graves, but it made no sense. If they wanted graves dug they'd have them dig their own graves and he'd seen enough of the countryside to know that graves were rarely afforded the executed. The desiccating sun and wind and the carrion eaters made short enough work of the shot and hanged. He listened intently to what they were saying, but he could not tell the language they were talking. He was not sure who they were or where their loyalties lay in this many-sided civil war.

As to the digging, his wonderings were answered for him when the pit was not so deep and they began dragging ammunition boxes from it and then a cache of rifles, a machine gun, and cartridge strips. They pulled wooden crates from where they'd been buried and they were marked with the same black letters as so many of the crates delivered south and stockpiled in the depot at expedition headquarters.

The crates of rifles and the machine gun and the ammunition retrieved, Napoleon and Preston were ushered to the edge and made to get inside the pit left by the digging. Then the young cowboy who'd attempted to parley before the battle approached them. He assumed from the start the boy was one of the Americans hired as dynamiters, machine-gun operators, soldiers of fortune.

"What are they singing about?" he asked the boy.

"Love, hunger, leaving home. What else is there?" the boy said, squatting at the edge of the pit.

"Not much, I guess."

"She wants to know if either of you is a dynamiter. They need one. Theirs was killed." Then he said, "She wants to know if you're one?"

"She who?"

"The one what runs this outfit."

"No," he said. "I don't know anything about the stuff."

"Have it your way," the boy said.

It was then Preston found his legs, rose to his full height, and said, "Would they consider a ransom?"

The boy gave him a funny look and then made a low humming sound in his throat.

"Listen," Preston proposed, taking out his wallet. "Tell them if it's money they want?"

Stupidly, Preston did not understand they would have his money whether he gave it to them or not, have it in whatever way they wanted to have it.

He told Preston to shut up and then to the boy, "You look kind of pale for this climate. What's your game?"

"I ain't going to ask you to live," the boy said. "Show them you know dynamite and you might be able to make it out of here."

"What about him?"

"I think they got other business with him."

"You mean you want me to show you," Napoleon said, daubing at his powder-grimed face. "That's your game, ain't it. You let your mouth write a check your ass can't cash."

"You shut your trap, you old peckerhead."

"You're supposed to be the dynamiter, only you don't know how."

"They're going to kill you."

"If they do, I don't think I'll be the only one they kill," he said, and with that the boy righted himself and stalked away.

Soon after that they were brought from the shallow pit and their hands tied behind their backs and they were made to kneel in the dirt. In defiance he lay down on his side and closed his eyes and his action became enough reason for Preston to topple beside him.

There came a distant commotion from the far side of the encampment, a marshalling of force and then it came on and was a kind of pageantry he'd rarely seen.

A white horse bearing a woman rider at a bridling gait hove up to the place where they lay. She wore her hair in a long black braid, a black fitted skirt and a white shirtwaist with a pearl gray suede vest. She wore a soft gray felt hat with an ostrich plume, pink-tinted glasses, and a pistol in a belt filled with ammunition. A braided leather quirt dangled from her wrist.

This was one of the recurring women riders he'd seen through the field glasses. He could see that she was an accomplished horsewoman and the horse bearing her was perhaps the finest he'd ever seen. The horse stood sixteen hands with a massive chest. It had a slightly convex face and large oval eyes. It wore a broad forehead and carried a long heavy neck, an abundant mane, and a thick low-set tail. Its saddle was embroidered with silver and there were silver cheek plates in the form of conchas on the harness. The horse was further adorned with a silvered face piece and breastplate. The tapaderas covering the stirrups were intricately silvered as well. It was an Andalusian, a purebred Spanish horse.

The woman's dress and manners and beauty, as well as the horse's, were high born. Napoleon took her to be from the wealthiest class and existing at a distance from the world, a distance that went beyond money and possession. In this land there were haciendas as big as a million acres. These were people with their own private kingdoms, their own private countries, and their own private armies.

Two Yaqui rode beside her in full war paint. They rode

matched golden duns with tiger eyes. They were hard beasts with dead eyes in their faces, the horses and the Yaquis. The Yaqui were tall and broad shouldered and they wore two bandoleers around their waists and two more across their naked chests. Riderless ponies dallied behind them with rotting heads impaled on the saddle horns. The heads wore long hair and in death their faces were crumpled with pain and their mouths shriveled and unmistakable smiles. Close by there was another woman who rode with them. This must have been the other woman he'd seen. Except this woman was a window manikin held upright in the saddle by a thin frame of steel. She too rode a fine white horse and was dressed similarly to the actual woman, a slant parasol puppeting above her head.

There was another who rode behind her. He wore a broad sombrero, silver-studded trousers, and a goatskin jacket. He was the one with the .45, its grips inlaid with mother-of-pearl and there were others in her party, their mounts gaunt, rough animals, with visible ribs and hip bones, but they were armed to the teeth and possessed the air of assassins. These other men had no politics. They were in loyal service only to the woman.

The boy came to them again.

"This is against the law," Preston said. It was a fatal part of his character not to bend at times, not to be pushed around.

"You want me tell her that?" the boy said.

"Yes," he said.

The boy went to her side and spoke to her. Then he returned to where they kneeled.

"She says she is the law," the boy said.

Before Preston could respond, the woman gave a signal and two men approached and dragged Napoleon and Preston onto their knees and roughly blindfolded them. He could hear Preston beside him, protesting his treatment. Then he felt the muzzle of a gun barrel at the back of his head. He tried to imagine another world where none of this was happening, but he could not. Preston went silent and there was silence at the ground and in the air. Then there was the sound of two triggers being cocked, one and then the other.

When the threat of death became imminent, Napoleon, like some men, extended an invitation. He felt daring, even hungry for it. He fell in love with the thought of it and wanted it as much as he wanted to live.

He could hear Preston again. He was whimpering.

Napoleon waited for his life to pass before him, not because he was afraid but because he was curious what it had all been about and also because he expected it. He expected the parade of his life, its events in quick succession to pass through his mind as complete and silent as a whisper. He felt the muzzle drag against his scalp, the result of a hard trigger or a weak hand.

"It's all right," he told the gunman. "Don't be nervous."

The muzzle shook and waggled as two-handed the man pulled the revolver's trigger. He wanted to reassure him.

"Do a good job," he said, waiting, anticipating.

Time crawled by. He could hardly breathe. There was a wind and dry dust lifted and was carried in the darkly moving air. He consigned himself to death, endured his wait. He thought of his brother, his father, his mother. Then he became aware of a sound rising up from his chest, the sound of a cry.

He made the one sound as if drawn from his throat and then no more.

He waited and waited for his life to be ended, but it was not and then there was the snap of a dry fire, the steel hammer collapsing on an empty cylinder. It was then his belly burned with what felt like boiling water. A roar went up and there was laughter all around and loud cheers.

He knew to smile and he could do no other than to let his head go back on his neck and laugh with them. It was a dirty joke but a joke nonetheless.

The man behind him clapped his ears viciously. It was as if his body had been struck by lightning instead of flattened hands. He could not hear and he could feel as his body was stripped naked.

The woman sat her horse and watched as they were hung from a live oak by their wrists and beaten with a heavy wet rope until he had little feeling left, his flesh so shocked there was only the thud of dull impact. She smoked a cigar while they were beaten. He could smell the drifting smoke and when he could smell it no longer that was the end of their beating and they were cut down.

13

PRESTON WAS LYING on the ground beside him. He was crying in a ragged, tortured, unstoppable way. His tears were burning down his face and choking in his throat. His body convulsed with each wracking sob.

Napoleon lay beside him, dry with the source of pain his own body had become.

Was this the same night of the strange morning of the night before? The morning they rode across the land while the sun was flat on the earth line?

He spoke to the sobbing man harshly, quietly.

"Shut up, god dammit," Napoleon said quietly. "Quit your bawling. You are killing yourself," he told the nerve-shattered man.

"I can't help it," Preston said.

"They won't pity you," he told him. "You are embarrassing them and yourself and they'll hate you for it and then they'll have to kill you."

"I don't want to die."

"It ain't your call," he said, and then his own pain-ridden mind thought, You poor gone bastard. But why did he care? There were so many things he did not care about anymore.

And then in his next thought, I still got a chance. You always had a chance until you were dead. The thought was involuntary and he did not like having it. It was best to not think at all and to let the mind that resided within the mind do the necessary thinking that led to action and then he could think about what he'd done later.

Against the night's darkness the white flames of the cook fires flagged in the wind. He lay bound and naked and contorted in that high place and was as if cast to an outer rim of a cold, waterless world. Shapes crossed before the cook fires and the fires disappeared and then the fires appeared again. How silent and beautiful the scene of the crackling fires. The civilization of the fires was as if the only civilization on the land and he was cast from it into a world starkly terrible.

They were being watched over by little boys, barely able to hold the shotgun they passed on with each changing shift. The little boys wore sandals and white cotton britches knotted with rope at the waist. They wore blankets and castoffs and all manner of headgear. One of the boys wore magenta-colored socks with his sandals.

There were hard flowers. What kind they were he did not know. The little boy who wore the magenta socks picked a handful after he handed the shotgun to the next little boy.

A man he'd not seen before came forward. He wore a broad-brimmed black sombrero, a red blanket serape against the cold night and striped pants worn tight. His face was pitted with pox scars. He had one good eye and the other was sealed behind a closed lid. The man moved with the ease of a predator and as if he possessed an ability to see in the dark, his movements subterranean. He threw back his serape. Un-

derneath he wore a brown suede jacket with silver embroidery
and in his hand was a knife, thin bladed with a white jigged-
bone handle and nickel silver bolsters. Napoleon watched the
man sidle up to Preston, who was naked and shivering in the
cold, his hands tied behind his back with twisted rawhide.
The man held the knife loosely in his hand. Napoleon could
feel his crotch shrinking as the man took Preston by his long
hair, pulled back his head, and raised the knife.

When the knife descended Preston's body convulsed. His
limbs flapped. He let back his head as if complicit in his own
maiming and then he moaned.

The work of a knife is quiet. The moment was suspended
as if a universal suspiration of all encompassed time and then
his screams rose up and split the darkness and were piercing
to hear as if unloosed was a bright dramatic and horrible pageantry. As sound after sound was torn from Preston's lungs
something like the taste of copper pennies filled Napoleon's
mouth and his eyes rolled up in his head. There was nothing
he could do to help Preston. He surged against his bindings,
quaking rigid in every joint, and then his body went slack. It
was useless. The one with the lost eye stepped away from the
bent figure and he watched as Preston's eye blood watered the
sand.

"I'm dying," Preston said. "I'm dying."

He could only imagine the desperate terror in Preston's
heart, or had he passed through the terror and now he was on
the other side where he was being cared for, the long-standing
promise made to the suffering by the loving Christian god?

"Not yet, god dammit. Not yet," Napoleon said.

"I am going to live."

"You can make it," he said, but he didn't think it.

Preston bent up painfully into a sitting position and then he stood. There was only blood where his eyes used to be.

"How bad is it," he asked before he could stop himself.

"I can still see you," Preston whispered, his nerves sending false signals to his brain, and it made Napoleon regret even more asking the question. "I can still see you," Preston cried.

Napoleon closed his own eyes and on the inside of his eyelids there was a dancing light, liquid red at first, as if seeing blood through water and then yellow and then white.

"I can see you," Preston said more loudly, and Napoleon told him to shut up, but he wouldn't. He kept saying it until the one with the lost eye came up behind him and kicked out his legs, knocking him to his knees. Then he held the barrel of the pistol to the temple of his head and without pause pulled the trigger and fired a bullet across Preston's face. When Preston fell forward he thought him dead, but he wasn't. The aimed bullet had not entered his skull but crossed his face in front of his brain, shattering the bones that rimmed his eye sockets, the fragile bones contained within his eye sockets, and destroying his nose bridge and his blue eyes.

The side of Preston's face was blackened where the muzzle flash burned his skin. There were shards of bones and pulverized bone floating in his head. He started bleeding again from the holes where his eyes used to be, as if the blood of a man was infinite.

Preston went silent for a long time. He lay on the ground and did not move. He thought him perhaps dead and gone, whatever light left inside him cold and extinguished. Then he could hear a whimpering sound and then words.

"I can still see you," he said.

"No," he said softly. "It's time for you to go."

The one who carried the knife with a white jigged-bone handle and nickel silver bolsters came again from the darkness to where they lay. He was eating an apple and the little boy was with him. He looked down at Preston, gibbering incoherently on the ground, and then he held the apple he was eating by his teeth while he unsheathed the knife and took Preston by the hair.

"Please kill me," Preston cried. "Please kill me."

The apple still held in his teeth he took Preston's face in his hands and when his hands came away he threw Preston's tongue on the ground. Then he sheathed the knife and went back to eating his apple and Preston never made another word.

As the night wore on the people walked out to look at the work that'd been done to them, the old women, the women nursing infants, the children. They came in twos and threes and they looked and then they turned away and walked back to the fires.

Napoleon did not know his fate, but he knew he was witnessing the destruction of the handsome man. For what seemed hours he could hear Preston suffering in the darkness. Something inside the man demanded an epic life and now he'd found it.

Then there came a stirring from around the fires. They brought forward a skittish mustang, hobbled and blindfolded, and a man stood at his head soothing it and whispering into its flicking ear. They dragged Preston from the ground and held him erect as they knotted his hands into the mustang's long tail. When this work was done the man with the lost eye signaled with a nod of his head and the hobbles were quickly removed, the blindfold pulled away.

The mustang tossed its head, sending a strand of slobber into the air. It shivered its body, as if an act of collection and self-determination and then it exploded, its hooves shearing into the man tied to its tail. The first kick was to the groin, him being so tall, and it crushed into him and before he could crumple the second kick was similarly placed and it tore away his privates. He cried out with a tongueless mouth. His cry was strangled and silent, as if the last desperate prehistoric cry. He'd not had time to fold between kicks, but now he folded and groaned and his mouth gaped silently. Both of his legs were broken and splayed from beneath him at cruel angles. The next kicks planted the hooves in his chest. They crushed his sternum and destroyed his heart and broke open his skull.

For Preston it was now over, but the mustang continued its kicking until what was tied to its tail finally tore away and then, exhausted, it settled and they led it away.

Walking on his knees, in the moonlight, Napoleon found the body of Preston, shot and whipped and stogged and kicked to death, and lay beside it.

His was a dirty death, but in the end it was his own death and no one else's and it'd been waiting here for him all these years and now he'd walked into its chain and it'd taken him in its embrace. He'd died long and hard in the unlikeliest of places. In America, he was someone, but in Mexico, he wasn't anybody. He'd cried and blubbered and tried to ransom himself with a wad of new folded greenbacks. He'd pissed himself and shat himself and his skin was saturated with runnels of blood and greasy sweat.

On the whole he'd been a vital young man of action who thought it was better to do something than nothing and to act wrongly was preferable to not acting at all. He wanted adventure. He yearned for a challenge. He desired risk. He'd been faithfully judged by the laws of war and it was determined he cross the threshold between life and death with no return.

Napoleon was so cold he began to crawl in the direction of the fires obscured by the shadows. The little boy walked along beside him lugging the shotgun. He reached the outer ring of warmth and when he felt this first heat he stopped and lay back. He stretched his neck and turned his face to the breathing warmth. The women were cooking frijoles. There was a crying baby. Then they began to let the fires go out. There was the sound of tack and tin pans and wooden boxes slapping shut as they broke camp in preparation for a night move.

They came to him and dragged him to beside the corpse. Weak and disoriented he'd never felt his body so old in motion.

"Your man is dead," the boy said to him.

"He weren't nothing to me," he said.

"She wants you will tell the others what happened here so they will know. She says you're only a soldier and you want nothing. You ain't got no other reason to be here and nothing to prove."

"Tell her she can go to hell."

"It would probably be best if I didn't."

They draped him over a hollow-backed bay, bound and

trussed him at the wrists and ankles. He felt the horse's hind-quarters flex and adjust to sustain his weight. Someone hit the horse across the crupper and they rode him away from that place for how long he did not know. He was as if baggage, and the walking steps of the horse entered him and dulled what little bit was left of him and his mind emptied.

They followed a steep trail through the pines and then began a long descent. For how long he had no memory. He was lost and upside down and seeing in the darkness of his own mind. He had no need to think foolish incantations. He'd already crossed over to the other side of thinking. He'd already released himself.

He remembered, that night, traversing a precipitous bluff cut by a deep arroyo running well back into the upper plain. Then they descended the bluff, crossed a dry river and pushed on through the darkness. At some point in the night they stopped and for a few moments he was conscious before passing out again.

Then his wrists were cut free from his ankles and with a shrug the horse shed him onto the hard desert floor where he lay naked on his back. His body was too sore to endure. When the horse moved on again it was pulling a long rope and Preston's body was dragging behind and then was a column of pack animals and then nothing.

14

THE NIGHT WAS STILL as a wing. There were traces of silent birds in the sky silhouetted against the halide moon, the full buck moon when back home the new antlers of the buck deer were in velvet. He lay on the hard stony plain beneath their overpassing flight. He was alone and cold lying so near to freezing on the ground, the Milky Way's white light stretching from one horizon to another. Out here he knew his entire welfare depended on the condition of his horse and to be without one was near fatal. He could die in this place, he surely could.

His mind went to the remembering place. He remembered home, his greenest days, waking up warm and hungry, the rooster nagging at the sun, the cow braying for relief from her engorged udder, a coal black horse stamping in a wooden stall. His mattress was smooth as a coated animal, the floor cold to his feet, and his hunger flaring inside him like an open hand.

His mother, Rachel, the morning her hair caught afire in the great kitchen when she leaned into the fireplace to retrieve a kettle. He and his brother were little boys eating their breakfasts, their spoons halfway to their mouths when she caught afire and before their eyes, she became a stalk of kill-ing light.

Every remembered thing left behind by the years but not that. It was not possible to leave that behind, no, not ever.

He wondered, Who left him here? He did not know. He knew there was a song they sang, the words "green as the sea were her eyes." One of the little boys who guarded him wore his color-tinted goggles, the little boy who followed him to the outer heat of the fires. He thought of the round-shouldered women sitting cross-legged on the ground, nursing their in-fants slung to their breasts, the women rising up with their babies and the women's spines bent back and the babies rising from their hips.

He saw again the horses, his brother would want to know: the golden duns with tiger eyes, the grullos, tobianos, and overos, a blue-eyed cremello, the majestic Andalusian the woman rode. The horses were as if from the distant and iso-lated kingdom of the circus where they were bred to be as illusory as the circus itself.

He thought of the fallen lying in last contortion, their dead eyes as they glutted the earth with their bright blood. He re-membered a man dismounting his horse. He threw his leg across the pommel and jumped down with a pair of alligator pliers. He'd stay behind to unclinch the nails and pull the shoes from dead horses. Man animals and horse animals, the hard beasts of the earth come to the place of the place of consequence and certitude. Whoever they were, they'd dis-appeared as if sewn into darkness and they left him where he was to fend for himself and he knew he would never see them again.

He knew the absolute silence of deserts, knew they were never really so, but this night was the most silent tent he'd ever experienced. The vault of the night sky curved overhead and was vast and empty as if a great hall where music used to play. The night was desolate, piercingly cold and made thin and transparent and he could see the stars and the stars behind the stars. The peace and beauty he felt he could not avoid, but it did not confuse him.

If it was pain that barred the door to death, then he'd had enough and he was ready. He closed his eyes and opened them as if to change the page of thought and find another scene, but he could not. He was in the time and place where he was and could fall no further than he'd already fallen and yet inside he could still feel something.

He thought, Extra Billy was an awfully good man and Bandy, with time, might have worked out too. His heart emptied at the losses he'd sustained and there on the desert floor he grieved over the so many fallen men of both sides in the battle and for a time all feeling he'd buried deep inside came to the world. He wept and his body was racked.

The night darkened, a dim invisible veil fallen across the scene and soon was a ghostly blue topography, as if a great understanding of his grief. He searched through the tenebrous darkness for the heartening light of the far bright star. He wished to lift a hand, to locate, but he could not.

Something was telling him this stony place where he lay would not be his deathbed. He wondered if perhaps Bandy made it too and was following the compass home.

What of the Rattler horse that saved his life? Would he ever know?

It was an immense dark night on earth and he felt to have been washed up on a high shore of the world. Whatever dim veil fallen across the heavens was lifted and again there were infinite stars spangling the blue night. The stars were faint and flickered gently as if alive.

How frail is the force that holds one on earth, he thought. How fragile the essence called life. In this cold starry place he was the only flicker of what is named human.

"Feeling bad?" he asked himself.

"I've felt better," he replied.

It was now the brightest heaven he looked into, as if the moon had impossibly increased. The silence was warm and deep and as if left by a sweeping hand. They liked the men to ride at night because they could not see their horses and it made them sit upright. The darkness also made the horses careful. At night they lowered their heads and released their back muscles. They became more alert, sure footed and obedient. On nights like this he would stop the horse and lay back and look at the stars, the haunches moving under his back. It is so like humans to think there is more out there than there is here. They are greedy for the water to be more and for the land to be more and even greedy for the sky to be more.

They left him in the center of a vast nothingness and still he could not understand why. He could not piece it out with his thoughts and his mind into a thousand parts was divided. They came at his heels as whispering crooked figures. Why had they left him wildered and not dead? Why had they not killed him? Tell the others, she told him. Tell the others what happened here.

When they rode out, they rode over him, the pack animals

in column stepping gingerly and their hooves passing to either side of his body, or carelessly stepping on his back and legs and arms folded over his head. Behind them they dragged the body of Preston, the last of their killed.

His mind had left his body and fled somewhere it might be safe until it could return and now it was returning. He was above the plain, as if hovering, his back to the earth. He tried to remember how he got there in case he had a chance to get back so he could tell his brother, but he had no way of knowing and could not remember.

He thought, I cannot bear what I have experienced, and then he thought, I can bear what I have experienced. He thought of the General. Not long ago the General lost his wife and his three little girls in a fire. Where before he had been a spare, alert, and jaunty man, he was now a caved and silent man, suffering insomnia and melancholia, living the lonely isolation of his personal grief.

He tried to remember how long he and his brother had been with the General, but he could not.

After that he slept for a while, or rather, there were long intervals in the night when he was not conscious. When he did awake, something doglike was standing over him and was sniffing him, its breath hot and sour.

"Go away," he whispered. "Shoo." He tried to lift a hand to wave it off, but he could not.

Then it went away but not too far. It went away to the edge of a circle where it joined other animals that he understood were watching him. Whether true or not, this was the impression he had.

He knew most snakes avoided the daylight and the heat

of the sun by prowling at night. He had the passing thought they'd be coming for him and already he was residing in a sea of rattlesnakes. From behind a stone a scorpion was looking at him, its spiked poisonous tail arched over its back. He could not help but feel this was all a dreadful mistake and maybe did not even happen.

He tried to move his body, but he could not. In the moonlight ancient trails would reveal themselves and on these he would follow to water in the morning. There were thorns about his head and his body and every time he moved they stung his skin. This was okay, the sensation of pain, because he felt it throughout his body and so was not broken or paralyzed. There would be time to move later, but for now he needed not to move.

He finally found sleep and in the secret whispers of memory dreamed himself home and was walking in cool sparkles of wet sunlight. The song of a wood thrush came to him from deep in the forest. His mother wore her white muslin morning dress and button shoes. She carried a parasol and a wide-brimmed straw hat, a daisy flower in her hair. She had packed a picnic basket in which she placed chicken salad, a jar of lemonade, hard-boiled eggs, pickles. There was a profusion of grapevine, dry and brittle, where they followed a short path and the wild roses were still wet with the morning dew, even though it was approaching noon.

As he walked the narrow path, she slipped in behind him, her hand up to fend off any branch he might let go, but he held each for her to pass by. There was a faint breeze on the air and pale yellow sunlight dappled the thin worn path they followed into the woods, but for all the light they found themselves surrounded with an indescribable aura of haunting loneliness. At the water's edge was a host of ruby-spotted damselflies. He slid his hand into the cool current until it was wrist deep. Above them a flat sheening waterfall fell from the rocks and tangled and the scattering water was dazzling in the sunlight.

His mother touched her hand to his smooth cheek. A tiger swallowtail lighted in her hair. There was an emotion he could feel that he'd never felt before and not since. He took off his shoes and socks and trousers. He wore his shirt to the water's edge as if shy and then discarded it at the last moment before plunging in. He swam to the bottom of the pool and looked up at the sky where sunlight was flashing its gold and silver on the water surface above his head.

15

WHEN HE AWOKE were pink traces of morning. The sun was breeching the horizon. A thin aqueous light was appearing in the east. The vein of light expanded and then was a snap of light and the sun risen and he lay in a parlor of sun, the shining tracks of virga filling the sky, lifting and decorating the sunlight, the magnificent structure of light all around him.

He was lying naked in the center of a vast playa, a dry flat lake bed. He was wrecked in a godforsaken place. This was not the land of humidity and decomposition, but the place of the sun shriveled and the dried-up. It was the vast dusty hollow of a bowl-like valley where he lay and surrounding him were endless miles of sand and windswept earth, high blue mountains, and deep ravines. He knew this land like the palm of his hand, but this day he had no idea where he was. He tried in vain to roll over, to stretch his hand beyond his body, but he could not.

His years on earth became dreamlike to him, a flash of moments experienced and without chains of interlocking experiences. When he remembered he did not see himself, but saw what was before him when it was before his eyes. For all that he'd experienced he was not there but was here and was the watcher and seeing it in his mind and placing it in his memory without remembering all the way to now and now was the only time that mattered.

And, for now, he had to keep what small life he possessed inside himself. He could not let it leave his being. He knew he would be found. His brother would travel in violence to find him. His brother would not give up, not ever, and for that reason he had an obligation to be found or his brother would search the desert until he died.

So, he determined, it was his duty to be found and his brother would find him. Or First Sergeant Chicken. Or Ten Square. Or Teddy.

If Teddy couldn't find him, nobody could. Teddy's conviction in pursuit, was like the hunting dog, efficient, alert, single-minded. He was an Apache. As a little boy he stood with Victorio at Tres Castillos. Seventy-two were killed and two hundred wounded were left to die. The rest: men, women, and children were rounded up and with lassos around their necks were marched into Chihuahua and paraded though the city with Victorio's head on a lance. Then they were marched to a reservation north of the international line.

The Apache used no map, no compass, no star to guide them. He could not figure it out for the longest time until he began to understand they were never lost because they never came from anywhere in the first place and were never going anywhere in the end. They were the place they were in.

It made sense to him, the anciently nomadic and wandering. If you were in a place where you did not belong, then you died, and after thousands of years the only ones who were left alive were the ones who were always where they belonged. He'd have to ask Teddy about this theory when they found him. He'd asked the Apache before and every time he did they only laughed. So complete were they in their being they did not even understand the questions he was asking them. In their language, they possessed no equivalent for the word lost.

If Xenophon did not find him, he would be so angry. Lord knows what he would do. He would scour the entire world and would not stop even after all hope was without and Teddy too would never give up, because Teddy was their friend.

"By God," Napoleon cried out, his mind unraveling inside his head. He knew he was about broken and needed to find what small piece of him that was still whole or he would perish and if he did—his brother would be so angry with him for being the reason an intention went unfulfilled.

By some effort he sat up. He looked for a sign, whatever sign he could find, however slim and without hope it might be. There was a bird flying west and the earth seemed inclined that way. West was the closest outcropping of rock. Where there was rock, where a bird flew, there could be a seep of water.

If he was to make it through this day, his mind would have a lot of convincing to do. He was naked and streaked with dust and covered with sweat and blood. His flesh was torn and deep bruises were rising beneath his skin. He needed to get more dusty if he was to survive the rays of this day's sun and the intensifying cold of another night. He touched at his umbered skin, how hot it already was.

He saw his hat not far off, in the same direction as the bird flew. For some reason they'd left him his hat. It was their joke, their invitation to him. It was the chance they afforded him and his slimmest hope. He took it as a sign that it could be done with only this hat the slightest edge.

He scraped away at the earth's surface with his bare hands until he found the cooler earth beneath. He dusted his skin with handfuls from head to toe, trying to mask his naked skin from the sun. He stood precariously and shook himself. It was a motion he regretted as it caused a slopping inside his head that dropped him back to his knees. His head was heavy and leaden and he was dizzied. His body never weighed so much before. He let himself down onto his hands and knees. His mind whimpered with signals to stand, to move a foot, a hand, to keep his head from lolling on his neck. He tried to make words, but he could not. Whoever struck him the blows to his head struck him that hard.

He stood again and walked over to his hat and by habit he kicked it before picking it up. Who knows what might have crawled under it during the night? He discovered they'd left him another item of his person, the holstered .45 and a single chambered bullet. The decision was his to make.

His only fear was dying alone and, until now, never by his own hand. This concern he confessed to himself this morning, but now he understood—you always die alone.

He drew relief from this. He told death he was ready and had no fear and inside was the preknown of his mind, was the kindling of an innocent curiosity about the life of death, the state of one's death existence and then it flamed and he was desperately curious about the end of this life and the beginning of the next one. He understood he did not care any longer and he took this as a good sign.

No matter, he had to get off this griddle before he burned away. His body was as if lit and transparent with its whiteness and prey to the sun's lighted rays. He touched at his burning skin, how hot it was. He had to move in a direction before the sun poisoned his head and burned his body and killed him. He needed to make it to the low sullen mountains to the west. These are the things he told himself to make himself stand up.

Erect and unsteady, he held himself at the vertical on his wavering legs. His head split with dizziness and ribboned light and gorge rose into his throat.

Lead with the left foot, he told himself. The left foot is the leading foot.

He took the first step and fell to his knees and keeled forward, groaning and scraping his face. He stood back up and this time he did not wait but took a step and then another step and he began to walk again.

Double-time, he thought into his legs. Thirty-inch steps. One hundred and eighty steps per minute.

Quick-time cadence, he thought. One hundred and twenty steps per minute.

Under that cloudless sky the earth heated until overhead the burning sun was as if intent on melting the everything beneath. What little fluid his body sweated he desperately licked from his palm and swabbed with dirt to darken his skin. Still, his skin baked as the sun shot its long bars of light from that cloudless blue sky.

His wounds were awakened and became heated knots on

his back and every time he tried to move, ever so slightly, his head pounded with the drum of pain.

Who was the great magician who struck this heat? He could go no farther. He found the faint hourglass of a shadow and lay down in its darkness among the creosote bush. As the shadow emptied and filled he rested and then he got up and moved again, ever closer to the high overhanging rocks in the distance. He would go until he was up against them and their stark barren walls clipped off the sun and there would be water and soon the nighttime would overtake the day and there he would find relief.

He sighed deeply, his mind not yet his own, but less disconsolate. He'd decided he'd have a little more life to live this day. But the feeling did not last for long as the sun had already poisoned him. His roiling gut lurched and on all fours he heaved drily as if a dog retching grass. He wanted the pain to stop, wanted his mind to arrest what was involuntary and again assert itself over his body's continual motion. But his mind could do little to gain control and so finally, mercifully, it passed him out.

For a time he lay there unconscious in the sand and dirt as if driftwood and waiting to be washed off with the next tide.

Then he got up again and trudged on. He was thirst on legs. His feet were shredded of nerves and had ceased their torment, no longer translating pain into his legs. They'd gone numb from the burn and the cuts, the thorns and slivers, they collected with every step. He'd walked and ridden and sailed the whole world. What was a night, a day, a night, however long before his brother found him? Breathless and faint he kept on in his direction. Far off and high up in the sky were the delicate strands of virga. It was raining up there but would evaporate and never reach the ground.

He went down on his knees in the dry dust, his lungs gasping for air. His eyes burned with dry tears and he made fists with his hands, clenching them and releasing and clenching again. He wondered on the winged horse that pulled the golden eye of heaven. He thought how his brother would love to ride that horse on its daily reckless flight.

By an effort he made his way onto his legs again. The sun's radiant light was coming from all directions. The sun's rays came directly into him or reflected off the ground. He felt them on his skin and in his eyes and they strained and his eyesight weakened. He was so tired, but he knew he had to find shelter. Through the heat shimmer rising off the desert floor he could see the mountain range so close. He knew he had to get to those rocks and rest and then to the mountain range beyond. And so foot by foot he marched in the direction of the rocks. Where there are rocks there might be more rocks and where there are more rocks there is shade and there might be water splitting the rocks.

They didn't break him; they couldn't have. They broke him; they must have. He sought the strong force that always resided within him and he always depended upon, but he could not find it. Staggering, dazed and vacant eyed he stumbled in what direction he did not know. His lips and tongue were swollen, his feet like dead stones at the ends of his legs. He felt the ebbing of his muscular strength. His weary joints gave way and he went down on his knees. Then he walked on his knees. He felt himself to be crossing a field of burning broken glass until he fell forward and then he was stranded on the burning glass. I will die alone, he thought.

"Stand up," he whispered. "Stand up."

"I can't," he said.

Then he heard his father's voice calling his name. It came full and complete as if a wind behind it. Not a wind, but something, and he looked around.

The westering sun in the smoke blue air was sad and terrifying and the changing image night was closing in on the eastern horizon. With darkness would come a moment of relief and then he would fight against the freezing cold. He heard his father's voice again saying his name. His father was telling him what he could not remember, but he knew it was his father and he knew the words he was saying, but he could not remember them.

When he woke up he knew his father had been with him. It was twilight and a full moon was rising in the southeast. The slanting light was slowly giving way to the moon's vast rising and milky umbra. With the gathering murk of night he pulled himself from his sandy den and stood erect. A dry prickly heat spread through his body. In the half light he stared into the distance. He watched for birds in the sky. Waited for the slimmest pattern to show the direction to water.

Soon he would be on the night side of the earth. He'd find his way. He'd begin to walk again.

It wasn't long before the sky was fully dark and the moon so bright it washed the sky and the white and spangled Milky Way was made invisible.

He took his bearings in the sky. Almost straight overhead

he found the bright star Vega and with Deneb and Altair he made the Summer Triangle. In the east he found the Pegasus, the winged horse, and to the northwest, the Big Dipper was rising from the horizon line. When he was a boy the Big Dipper was always visible, but in Mexico it rose and set nightly.

He found Polaris, the North Star, the far bright star, where every night it sat nearly still at twenty-five degrees above the northern horizon. True north he calculated and in his mind he saw the map grid. There were 17.7 miles to a degree. He needed east and he needed north and he needed west. In his mind he saw grid east and grid north and grid west. Overhead the glinting stars were fixed in the heaven. He was cold, but he'd have to keep moving.

"I'm ready," he told his father, and his father heartened him.

He looked again to the moon and how strange it was. It was as if a little bite had been taken from it. Then, slowly, more and more of the moon grew darker until after a while three-fourths of the lunar disk was deep in coppery eclipse. The Milky Way revealed itself and he could see the great star clouds of Sagittarius. After that the umbraled moon began to reclaim its round shape and it grew again and the Milky Way faded away.

Beneath the star-scattered sky, he began walking again.

16

THE BEGINNING OF the next day brought the red-necked vultures. They stood away in their watch but close enough he could see their black flitting eyes. A creeping murmur came from their wattled gravelly throats, a sad gesture that made the rounds and then they silenced again. He would be their food. They had all the time in the world.

The ball of fire that was the sun loomed on the horizon. He was lying on a rocky stretch of ground. He'd gotten himself this far, but from where and how much farther was his destination? So like a man to wake up where he didn't know and didn't remember and still think it progress.

He felt himself, his senses, alternately sharp and then dull. For a time his vision disappeared and he could not see and when his sight returned he looked across a vast open area of complete emptiness. He was experiencing a burning unendurable thirst and try as hard as he could he could not remember when last he had a drink of water. His chin sank to his chest and he staggered. His mind was growing confused — he knew. He swept his eyes over the whole horizon. A shimmering vision of water rose in the path of his destination. As the sun climbed higher, the illusion evanesced.

We only have one death to break through to enter the eternity of all time, he thought. Just one death and then we are free forever.

I must live, he thought. I still think I can and I still think there is a reason to.

He was closer to the rocks he'd seen yesterday, but yesterday's effort had taken a terrible toll on his being. He could not remember when yesterday was.

Just lie quiet, he told himself. Find something to think about.

It was a time not so many years ago, crossing the Lolo Pass and stopping and squaring the Rockies with his thumb and forefinger. One of the jerk-offs joked about pissing on the Divide, whether he wanted to piss in the Atlantic Ocean or the Pacific.

"Because you know," he said, "from here it goes one way or the other."

Those were the good times with the last of the old hands, wild horses, wild cattle, lions, wild hogs. Still some grizzly roaming at night under a forest of stars.

He remembered the ride over the Divide, the steep rocky trail into the beautiful and wooded high country, the tall pines, oak, cedar, and juniper. The quaking aspens. They campaigned at seven thousand feet in storms of hail and snow. What he would trade for a little of that cold right now.

He climbed onto his legs and began walking. He stopped and sniffed the air for the ripe smell of water and then continued on through the brittle scrub. He was sorely tired and knew he had to stop eventually, but he also knew sleep was a black hole from which he feared he would not recover and so he staggered through the boundless emptiness like a drunken sleep walker. He continued on toward the low sullen mountains. He had no mind to divert his attention, no mind to receive the delivered news of the pain he must have been feeling.

He suddenly felt the presence of a stranger beside him and avoided his gaze, turning his head, not looking into his eyes. The stranger was beside him, or behind him and only his shadow was cast to prove his presence. But to turn to him, to look at him would mean death. It would mean to be taken in his embrace and gentled from this place, this earth and into another. He did not know how he knew this. He just did.

"I'd rather not go just yet," he said to the stranger.

For all the horror of this world it was still his own and he was not done and he'd not give himself over. He began to beat his arm as if swatting a fly, a bite, an affliction of the skin and deep in his throat sourced a keening wail, the jabber of the insane, and the stranger was driven back for the time.

But why not go with the stranger? He touched at the .45. Why not speed the death that would be the transition? Why not give up the pain, the injury, the slow and terminal? He worried and fretted how cool his skin had become. He understood how at the end a freezing man felt alive with heat and a drowned man could breathe and a burning man became cold and shivered and then died.

Why live when you could die? Who can answer that question and have the answer not be the selfishness you feel for the life that is your own?

He understood God to be fierce and prideful and taunting and these were the aspects of himself that God made in man. In his secret mind he speculated that worship and prayer and prostration offended God and made him weary. The daily freight of the thousand-million prayers rising from the hulled earth and converging on God's ears must have filled God with loathing and disgust so long ago, all those simpering, greedy prayers.

Each time he stopped to take his bearings the mountains seemed to have moved. He could not tell if he was headed toward them or headed toward their ghost image refracting in the warmer air above the desert floor. He sat down and rested his head on his knees, his arms holding his legs. He listened to the murmuring air and the sifting land, the profound stillness of this outer landscape.

He knew his brother would kill to find him. Nothing would stop him.

He closed his eyes and when he opened them, he stood, he adjusted accordingly and he continued on his slow torturous path.

It was then he understood why they let him live. It was to haunt the others, to confuse them, to tell them what happened to him. They let him go back because he would not be good for the others in any way. His living would confuse their minds and sow discontent.

Maybe he wasn't worth killing. He took only mild offense at the thought. What did he care? He was grateful for their disdain.

He arrived at consciousness to the sound of beating wings. He'd been walking unconscious, unaware that he was even walking. He heard his father's voice again, as if from a great distance come through the shield of heat and the dust and the noise the heat made inside his head.

Dragging a cross, on a desolate plain, he imagined the Jesus, blood dripping from his spiked crown. Inside he was drying up. He felt the touch of death and he began to not care if he lived and for a time this invigorated him. What was death to him? Just another unreal and meaningless experience.

He was now like the ghost of a ghost wandering.

Stiffen the sinews, summon up the blood. He heard these words. *Hold hard the breath, and bend up every spirit to full height.* His father was talking and had been doing so before he came to consciousness.

I am the lion in your blood—his father's words appearing in his mind and telling themselves to him and then vanishing and he could not remember them, but he knew it was his father.

He craned his neck and stared blindly into the sun. He remembered a spring in the pine timber country and another one that rose from the stony ground in little pools. How white and relentless the sky furnace. Sweating, panting, shivering out his life in the violent light he kept on.

He began talking to his mind and gently chastising it as if it were a recalcitrant child. His grandmother told him the blue darners were called the devil's needle because they sewed shut the eyes and nose and mouth of disobedient children. He wondered how much of the mind was only memory?

Then it was a seep he found, a dry rock wall he came to with a seam of water. From the seep a thin stream trickled into a calciformed stone that overbrimmed and lipped and disappeared. The water soothed his parched mouth and cooled his blood when he mopped his neck. He could not believe he found it and was on the verge of tears. At ease, he thought as he rested in shadow under the veil of rock where he'd found water like an angel.

At dusk the full moon began its rise in the crepuscular light and its glowing would last the entire of that night until it set at dawn. Tonight would be a moonshining night, the moon's light like cast fabric and so tonight maybe he would be found.

He let himself lie back, the .45 at his right hand. The heavens were on fire this night. The wide vessel of the universe was as if a land aflame with torches. There were stabs of fire in the sky, as if windblown, and he wondered what they were, each in their candlelike moment spectacularly magnificent. It was the kind of thing he'd have commented upon if he'd been with someone. He wondered if anyone else on earth saw them. He'd try to remember them to ask when he was found if anyone else saw the stabs of fire.

Then for a time the night was a belt of total darkness and a womb and there was infinite silence and the world took on the blackness of hell. Figures, indistinct and formless, wandered here and there in his vision. There came a period of thunderless lightning in the sky. At first the lightning meandered and striated and then broke to horizontal in fractured structure. The lightning beaded and pearled in long crackling chains that curled and whipped. The strokes dissolved into countless luminous segments and long lines of bright strands or exploded like rockets with splays of innumerable fingers. Then there would be a leader and another leader and leaders followed leaders. The leaders stepped and by return stroke in the opposite direction they established a channel that seemed to simultaneously pour down into the earth and return to the heavens.

Then what was happening up there stopped and the night returned to itself.

Perhaps there'd been a short war in heaven. A revolt of the saved and ascended and they wanted to come back down to earth and be men and women again and were sick of being God's angels. He wondered, Is it possible to capture some kind of truth before you die? To learn what is behind the surface and to learn the secret of everything that matters?

He held to the slender thread he was hanging by. He'd found water and now he'd live to be found by his brother. They say a man must have something to live for. Is being saved from death enough of a reason? Watch for a falling star. Make a wish it happens soon.

If I get that lucky I'll drink until I drown, he told himself. He thought about God and how he had exercised his overwhelming advantage and yet, he was still alive. This was the time for God to cut a deal if he was so inclined.

"Make me an offer," he throat-whispered. "If you want me, make me an offer, you son of a bitch."

That night he dreamed it was a very cold day and he remembered how much chilblains hurt after staying out too long, riding the toboggan with his brother.

Together they careened down the Copperhead Road, as if riding a thin margin of the world. The snow was blank white and banked in turns and when the road dropped they caught the air and flew and whumped down and he bit his lip, but it was so cold the blood froze on his chin. When they hit the bridge floor the rough slivered planks dragged them to a stop. Running beneath them were the white tails of fast moving water. They were looking at each other and seeing each other and without separateness, as if between them was the same miraculous power that holds water together. No two people can occupy the same space, the same event, the same moment, yet they did, and he remembered how beautiful the cast light in his brother's face.

Then they trudged back up the mountain and did it all over again until there was nothing left in their young bodies and they tramped home and curled up by the copper flames.

They were their father's boys and their mother's awkward animals. Cast in the parlor stove were lions' heads and there was a long wooden pipe that carried water to the kitchen from the hot spring. The water smelled of sulfur.

Their father said, "The cold is good for you," and their chilblains throbbing in their feet and hands and thin ankles, they fell asleep on the floor in front of the fireplace.

His memories were vague and gray. He heard a tap on a window blurred with rain. He saw the photo of a woman's oval face and a shocking abundance of black hair. His mother.

"I have had such awful dreams," his mother said. She was holding a biscuit cutter.

"People should be left alone," she said.

That spring the enchanted weather was wind running with banks of mist that rose in the hollows. Spring was a necklace of leaves and in summer he liked to feel the grass under his feet when he walked the plashy meadows and rambled the sun-swept hillsides, the coal black horses an otherness on the land.

They had two pet geese and the geese were blind. In the fall they set the blind geese in the upland pond where they swam and the geese called in the hour before daylight. They waited in a place in the trees called a blind, their faces bathed by a delicate mist, and when the wild geese flew in they rose up and shot them and that same night they ate them.

When he woke up it was still dark. He could feel a growing intimacy for the place he occupied. A scroll of traveling lightning wavered in the darkness.

"Is this the mystery of death?" he said, looking around, speaking his words into the vacancy and mumbling a reply and not remembering what he was talking about with himself.

"Are you all right?" he asked.

"I think so," he said.

"Your eyes?" he said, but to these questions he was asking himself he had no answers.

"Please don't talk," he said, feeling stiffness about the eyes.

"I never used to be afraid of dying."

"Me neither."

"It's not your time, I promise."

"Please, I just want to lie here and not talk."

"Then go back to sleep," he said.

However strange his lostness was to him he persisted in knowing he would live to be found.

Then the night sky spangled with milky light. It seemed to fall from the pallid stars as if poured from glass and all the way down to earth and he again allowed himself the thought he would make it, but with thoughts of the future were attendant memories of what happened in the desert and he could not keep them quiet in his conscience. He felt the weight of a knotted sorrow and however hard he thought it away, this heavy weight he could not lift from his heart.

He knew there would be more war because he knew by law of nature men would to war. All the young men were on fire to cross the ocean and fight. They were bloodthirsty for the blood that was not their own. Like little boys, they would have it and the old men would let them have it and it would turn out widows and orphans and heartbroken mothers. They would weep and moan for their husbands, fathers, and lovers. After the war was before the war.

17

WHEN HE WOKE in the morning the only sound was the husking of the wind. He imagined he was near the end of a dream and presently he'd awaken with a start and see the walls of his tent, hear the snorts of horses.

He lay on a sougan and a tarpaulin shelter rigged to block the sun. A wet cloth lay damping his forehead. He vaguely remembered the palm of a hand tilting his head and water wetting his face and leaking into his mouth, bathing his swollen tongue. His lips were wet and his face burned and cooled at the same time.

Teddy squatted beside him, his rifle held to his chest pointed at the sky. His back was crossed by bandoleers of ammunition, his one vanity a yellow silk binding his long black hair. A canteen sat in the sand easily within reach. A ways off his brother sat in a canvas chair he'd unfolded beneath a white cotton umbrella. He could see his brother's black boots. They were knee-high leather boots and he wore them with a woolen insert around the knee so they wouldn't rub.

His brother had a rifle across his lap and was eating canned salmon as he read a magazine. When he was finished he tossed the can, licked his spoon clean, and slid it into the

top of his boot where he carried it. He wet a finger with his
tongue, turned a page of his magazine. He then slipped sun-
flower seeds into his mouth where he cracked them with his
teeth and spit away their husks while he continued his reading. When his mouth was empty he reached into his pocket
and took out another handful of seeds and fed them into his
mouth.

However injured Napoleon might be he was not sure, but
he was contented and fulfilled and replete in the constancy
of his brother's reading and spitting, in the presence of Teddy
squatting beside him. He tried to say something. He was trying to get his thoughts right and fashion them into words, but
what do you say when you are born out of death?

They said nothing to him. They asked him no questions
and made not a sound. He later learned they'd ridden seventy
hours, day and night, without stopping. They started with a
cavvy of the best horses laddered behind them and changed
horses frequently, cutting the expended ones loose in the
desert. First Sergeant Chicken and Ten Square did the same.
Bowman, Goudge, Merrill, Little, Hubert, Fat Mouth, Gauly,
Taylor, and Wheeler all with supreme skill in the handling of
horses ferried out fresh relays as they sliced off vast reaches
of the high desert in search of the missing patrol. There were
now dozens of blown horses they'd discarded in their search,
dropped dead or still wandering the desert land.

They maintained a watchful gaze that passed over him and
into the beyond and would not presume to look at him for
how broken, burned, and undignified his being. His brother
and the Apache waited silently for a sign from him, so little of
what is called life was left inside him. They would've waited

the rest of that week if necessary and if he didn't recover only God knows what his brother might've done.

As far as he could tell, he lay in the middle of nowhere. He was aware of a presence, the wall of stone, the depression where he sheltered, but nothing else except emptiness. He reached with his hand and flailed to find the seep of water that saved his life, but he could not find it. The ground was hard and dusty and only rock and no evidence that it'd ever been otherwise. There was no water where he lay and the water he thought he found was made in the gentle mind that was easing him into his death. His mind was so like a ghost inside his head. He could feel the daggers of sunlight through the tarpaulin, death's hand still trying to touch him.

He groaned at the thought, so close it was, and Teddy turned and silently held a canteen to his lips and tipped it forward. The water trickling into his mouth seemed to need itself. He lifted a hand and tipped a guzzle into his mouth until he was choking and water was spiking in his nose. When he began to shake Teddy withheld more until he collected himself. Then he let him have a sip more.

"What day is it," he managed to say.

Teddy shrugged—how should I know? Why would I care to know?

"How long," he asked, meaning how many days gone by.

Teddy flicked three fingers in the air. Three days. That long.

He closed his eyes and opened them and when he did Teddy had turned away, the yellow silk an extraordinary color at the back of his head.

Teddy continued his vigil. He looked to his front and then

left and then right. It wasn't caution but habit. He was like the wild animal, stalking his prey while at the same time being preyed upon. Teddy held few illusions of innocence and experience, right and wrong. He was here and passing the time and coldly indifferent to both time and place.

"He murder anyone looking for me?"

Teddy looked at him and then away. It was a pointless question. We murder them or they murder us.

He knew he was safe. The Apache held sight beyond the horizon. His brother claimed their sight was 361 degrees and their vision took their sight over the curve of the earth. The Apaches were never found and never discovered. They did the finding. They did the discovering and when called upon they did the silent bloody work that was necessary.

For Teddy this life was just killing time until he could enter the next life and his paradise in the underworld where he'd live forever and never have to die again. There he would find all good and tasty things to eat and there would be water and there would be an abundance. In the underworld, life would go on much as it did in this life, but it would be a better life than this one because there would be no more meaning to comprehend. There would be no purpose, no reason, no significance, no concern. He'd scout and hunt and fight, but in the underworld these would just be something to do and unnecessary and what a relief that would be.

After a while he awoke to the sound of a horse riding hard. It was Sergeant Chicken. He rode a paint and behind him dallied another paint, a high-white, blue-black sabino. The horse was white stockinged to above the knees and wore a jagged white pattern on the belly and flank. There were white markings on its face that extended past its eyes. Later he would learn those eyes were blue. The blue-black sabino was a ghostly horse, its markings, as if an afterthought, half conceived, half executed. The horse was bone and wrung-out muscle and still it was a beautiful and, the way it carried its head, an equable horse. It made him think, What a pretty horse.

Sergeant Chicken leaned down from his saddle. He spoke to his brother and pointed to where he'd come from. Then, leaving the sabino behind, he hied off again in the direction from which he'd appeared.

The sabino looked down at his brother who'd resumed leafing the pages of his magazine.

It was a long time after that a wagon pulled by a team of mules, the swingletrees rattling and traces flying, trundled into the place where he lay. In the bed was a pallet of straw between square blocks of ice wrapped in woolen blankets. The many hands were then lifting him over the sideboards and settling him on the cooling pallet of straw. Over this they rigged the tarpaulin to keep him cool and keep out of the burning sunlight. When they lifted him he lost his breath as he felt to fly and only in shade did he catch his breath. How empty he felt the hollows of his bones, as empty as wind-blown ash.

His brother reached over the closed tailgate and gently clasped his head in his hands and their faces were so close. He looked up into his brother's suntouched face. His brother's eyes were blue and gray and sharp and his face as always was mask to his thoughts. He could smell peppermint.

With the touch of his brother he felt collapse the last structures inside him. He could still feel death's weight. It was the only feeling he knew. His eyes watered and he tried to speak but his brother gestured—you shouldn't talk.

"Where were you?" he struggled to say.

"Please forgive me. I am sorry."

"You are forgiven," Napoleon sighed, and then he said, "There was a time I didn't think I was going to make it."

"Sometimes you think it's special because it's happening to you, but it's not."

Then his brother told him it was waiting to happen and it would have happened to anyone, but it was he who was there when it happened.

"I am not dead yet, am I?" he said.

"Someday. But not yet."

His brother then told him how he was taking a nap when in his sleep it came to him that something terrible-bad was happening.

Napoleon opened his mouth to speak, but his jaw cramped and he could not close it.

"I knew right then," his brother said, easing closed his mouth, and told him he pulled on his boots and fetched the Apache and they began to ride.

"I knew you would know," he said.

"You're alive," his brother said.

"I don't know if you could call it that."

"I thought I lost you." His brother smiled.

His brother told how the meat wagons went to rendezvous and there was nothing there. They waited around and then the storm came and they barely made it back. But by that time he was already in the saddle.

"I am the only one?"

"You'll feel better after a cool bath and long drink," his brother said, but Napoleon made no response because he was not so sure that would be the case.

"Bandy?" he said.

"No sign."

"He had a chance," he said, and his brother shrugged. Maybe.

Overhead the sky was deep and from where he lay he could see the mountains blued in the distance. Fields of white cloud moved west to east shadowing the land. He put his hands in front of his eyes on the off chance someone should see him weeping for the grief and tranquillity, the stillness and humility he felt inside his mind.

By this time Sergeants Ten Square and Big Chow had converged on their location and the tarp was lashed secure. His brother stepped away, gave the order and the mule skinner called out. There was the rattle of harness and a jangling lurch and they were moving, and his brother and the Apaches took him away from there as if their business done and they owned all the time there was and every place it occurred.

In the days to come he'd tell his brother everything that happened. He'd tell him about the sandstorm and how they dismounted and formed a line and then came the blood horse. How Turner was shot in the guts and there was a double-barreled shotgun and that was the end of Turner, and Stableforth shot in the mouth and Extra Billy turning on the machete when a bullet cut him down. He'd learn there was no sign of the old man he'd doctored for gangrene and left to be found waiting by the road for the wagons.

"There ain't no albinos," his brother would say of the horses.

"That's what I thought," he would say, and his brother would think about what he said and after a while he would speak again and he'd say, "Extra Billy was kilt twice," as if it should not be overlooked or forgotten.

"The old man?" he asked again.

"I tell you there weren't no old man."

He would remember waking up in the Sibley tent, his bloody feet soaking in a basin of water. The light of a huge half-moon was crossing the pellucid darkness and graying the inside of the tent were the shadows of the passing men against its walls. There was an orderly breaking ice with a hatchet, crushing it and filling ice bags with screw tops. He was surrounded by them. He felt a hot flush run through him and then shivered from their cold. Beneath his cot were more cooling blocks of ice giving up their cold and melting into the thirsty earth. There was a watermelon in a washtub, a porcelain water pitcher and basin.

"What in hell?" he said, and the orderly looked up at him with wide anxious eyes. He tried to sit up but couldn't. He felt as if something was shattered inside him. He felt hot and cold and experienced a fit of hard-shaking chills followed by nausea.

"What are you doing?" he demanded to know.

"I was tol' to keep you cooled down and the flies off'n you."

"Find me some spurs," he said. "Saddle my horse." But he began to shiver again and could not stop himself and his teeth were chattering.

Outside the wall of the tent he could hear them talking.

It was said he ought to be dead is what he ought to be.

"How many was killed?" another voice said.

"All of them," the first voice said.

"It's a miracle he ain't dead."

"Yes. It's a fucking miracle."

He could smell the cigarettes they smoked and wished for one. Then he slept again. For how long he did not know. His body stank with sweat and burned dead skin. At least he knew he was not now dead.

18

THAT FIRST NIGHT sleep was difficult and spent in vague, deep, and inaccessible dreams. He knew he was at the depth of his physical decline and on the verge of his recovery. He began to shiver from the sun's poisoning and could not stop himself. Soon his whole body was quivering and his teeth clacking and he cried out for how painful the shuddering movement that racked his body. He felt himself to be coming apart with the force that struck his joints and could not help but cried out in agony.

His brother called to him, saying his name and he wondered where he'd heard the name before and then he recognized it as his own.

His brother left his cot and lay down on top of him, covering his body with his own as if to keep him from flying apart. He worked his arms around him and squeezed and held him, his face in his neck until the jarring shakes relented and he could collect himself. They came on again and swept through him with a ferocity that left him panting and helpless.

The repetition of the ordeal exhausted him and he had all he could do to smoke the cigarette his brother shaped for him. The strong black tobacco dizzied him and gave him some peace, but he could not help himself and he moaned with the slightest movement, with each return of the judders, and he knew his body would cry with ache in the morning.

From outside the tent came a light and the murmur of voices. A Coleman lamp had been lit and turned down low and two old troopers were smoking and drinking and remembering their horses. He fell to sleep again and passed into a second sleep and this one took him into the dead of night and through to morning. When he woke it was to the familiar hum and din of the army. He remembered waking in the desert and the yellow silk that bound Teddy's black hair. He remembered being lifted into the wagon, being held in the night in his brother's arms.

Teddy sat on a stool at the tent opening. The way his shoulders and arms moved he was working horsehair. He was content to lie still and watch Teddy's back, the weaving movements of his shoulders and elbows. When they brought fresh blocks of ice, Teddy picked up his stool and stepped aside with his flow of strands that they might haul in fresh blocks to place under his cot. He closed his eyes that they should think him asleep.

But Teddy wasn't fooled and sent for his brother and when he came he brought a cup of sweet sugary coffee, a waxed paper full of hot biscuits, and a basket of eggs. He unfolded the canvas chair and sat down beside the cot. He took out his tobacco and rolled him a smoke and after lighting it, placed it between Napoleon's lips.

His brother said nothing and in his presence there was no curiosity. There were no anxious questions as to the battle, the killed and missing men, or the days he experienced in the desert.

Napoleon held up a hand, a preface to saying something, and then he let his hand back down—the best he could do.

His brother leaned over and took his chin in the perch of his hand and studied his thinned and haggard face. Both Napoleon's eyes were blackened and his lips were split, crusted and swollen. His cheeks were raw and yellowed with blisters.

"I see you got scratched up pretty good," his brother said, but the only sign of concern he could read in his brother's face was the constant tonguing of a toothpick he chewed when he was not smoking a cigarette.

"You okay?" his brother asked, cocking his head to one side. "You ain't cuckoo?"

"Do I look okay?"

"No. You look like death warmed over," he said, letting go of his chin and sitting back in the canvas chair.

"I feel like it," he said.

"You made it," his brother said. "You get to do everything one more time."

"It's a regrettable thing."

"They were brave horses," his brother said.

"Bandy and Extra Billy," he said. "It is my shame to have lost those men."

The affair had been worse than tragic; it had been stupid. He needed to ease his heart. He could not help himself in this moment.

"I see your meaning well enough," Xenophon said, but still, he himself regretted more the loss of the mounts.

"I want to be dressed," he said, and heard his voice break like a child's.

After his brother helped him stand from the cot he held erect for some seconds and then with a groan he collapsed to the floor, upsetting the cot and the canvas chair, the coffee and biscuits. His collapse was so complete his brother could not catch him in his falling and he felt his cheek split open.

His brother kneeled down and righted the cot and lifted him to his feet that he could lie back down.

"Got any more bright ideas?"

"No."

Xenophon bandaged his bleeding cheek and washed him and put liniment on him to soothe his leg and arm joints.

"Bad things happen in this world," his brother said.

"Do you believe it will be any better in the next?"

"What next?"

Xenophon worked hard trying to make the pain come out of Napoleon as if his body was just another body to be worked on, like the body of a horse, but it was a stubborn pain he worked and not wholly of the body. If the pain was inside the mind it could be seen through the depths of the eyes, just like a horse. No one knew when or how the pain could get there, but a pain that found its way into the mind was to be feared the most because pain in the body was treatable and could be worked out of a man or a horse. But when the pain found its way into the man's mind, or the horse's mind, it was impossible to tell.

He lifted his head to watch his brother's attempt to relieve his body, to restore some peace to his aching bones and muscles and skin.

"They were not Villa's," he said.

"Why do you say that?"

"There were Yaquis with them."

"Then who were they?"

"I believe they were their own army themselves."

His brother was running his hands over him, finding the pain's hot joints and each time he did he made fists and sank them deeply into his burned flesh. Why he was doing this he did not know. The pain had no location and his skin was agony when touched. His face stiffened under his brother's heavy hands and more than once he moaned and had to catch his breath.

His brother paused and sat back and when he returned to his work his touch was lightened.

"That feels good," he said.

"No, it don't," his brother said.

From the basket his brother took an egg. He broke the egg and dishing the yolk from one shell to the next he let the raw albumen pour from the shells onto his burned skin where it smoothed and gelled.

"Try and sleep some more," his brother said.

"I have nightmares."

"What kind of nightmares?"

"I can't remember."

"Is it the kind of thing you want to remember?"

"No," he said. "Probably not."

"You'll take it to bed with you for a while," his brother said.

One after another he cracked the eggs and held the yolks inside their shells and let the cool albumen slide onto his skin and then he covered him with a thin clean sheet.

"Did you ever think of getting married?" Napoleon said.

"Did I ever say I did?"

"No."

"You marry a wife you have married trouble."

"That's what I thought."

That day and night there was a turmoil in his mind. He'd seen worse, he just couldn't remember when. But this time there was a sureness taken from him, a carelessness and a sureness when it came to his being. He could not explain it. He was still an able and confident man, but something had slipped away from him and left behind was an emptiness he could feel inside himself. He was entering into a new and strange life. Was it brought on by the unfortunate events in the desert, or was it waiting for him all this time and an experience and condition inevitable?

When he awoke, inside the tent was sably darkness. At first he was unsure of his surroundings, but then he recalled where he was. He remembered Extra Billy lifting a bloody fist to his smiling lips and tipping his fist as if a whisky glass. He shooed the thought away and another, shot through the jaw and his mouth a mixture of teeth and bone and flesh, the face skin blown open and the working muscles revealed.

On a plate beside his cot was a hamburger sandwich and there was a pitcher of water. His cheek felt tight and knotted. When he touched it he could feel coarse horsehair stitches where he'd broke it open. His brother or Teddy, both of them horse doctors, applying their needle and rough technique to his cut face while he slept.

He remembered a sheltered place with mud walls, an ancient place built on the ruins of an earlier civilization, a fairly well-traveled road, an approach to a mountain pass, but a place he had never been before. Such places are scattered across the deserts of the world, but where was this one? Could it be they went back in time and only he was allowed to return?

Arbutus howled from beyond the wall of the tent. He thought, What beautiful dreams the insane must occasionally have: the violin, the green apple, people who love each other, people who gaze hopefully, people who forgive, God.

He could make out his brother's form on the cot beside his own. He lay with his hands behind his head and made blue cigarette smoke. He rarely slept in his cot and usually slept with the horses.

"Are you awake?" Napoleon said.

"You're not dead yet?"

"No. Not lately."

"Good."

"Koons?"

"Koons? He died."

"Let me share that cigarette," he said, and his brother reached it over to him.

The memories began again to take him. He knew he died out there and when he died the old world died with him, but it made no difference because the new world would likewise be a world of killing and in most ways indistinguishable from the old world.

"Preston," Napoleon said.

"He was a complete bastard, that one. May he go to the hot place."

His brother lit another cigarette from the one they'd been smoking and they shared this one too.

"Now what are you thinking?" his brother said, spitting a fleck of tobacco from between his teeth.

"Nothing. I was just away in my mind." He shrugged his shoulders. The question meant little to him. There was no meaning in any of it.

"Can't remember?"

"No. Not really," he said, and it was true, he could not.

19

WHEN HE CAME from sleep it was in daylight and he was lying on his cot. He tried to think, but it was difficult and when he did he could not understand his thoughts. He closed his eyes to help his memory and for all there was to remember, he remembered nothing.

He opened his eyes again and his brother was sitting beside him as if just come in and Teddy was at the opening, several feet of a diamond-patterned macardy rope as if emerging from his thigh. He asked after the hand mirror and in the mirror he learned his eyes were shoe black and his stitched face gaunt and worn down as the predead.

In this moment he felt himself again to have returned.

"What o'clock is it?" he said.

"Maybe six."

"Which one? The first or the second."

"The second one," his brother said. He'd been to the Chinaman in town to drop off their wash and brought back chop suey and chowchow and chopsticks to eat with.

"Where's the whisky?" he asked.

"Right here," his brother said, holding up a bottle.

"I got a bastard behind my eyes."

"There's candy for you," his brother said, shaking the bottle by the neck.

"Give it here," he said.

"You want that on the rocks?"

"Yes."

His brother chipped ice from under his cot and poured the whisky into glasses.

"God, that's refreshing," Xenophon said, taking a drink from his own glass as he passed the other. "Drink that," he said. "It'll make you feel better."

"What kind of ice is that?" he asked, holding the glass up to the light and seeing through its amber transparency.

"I believe it's the kind made with water."

"Water?"

"Water that has been frozen."

"What'll they think of next?"

He took a deep drink, the liquor sluicing his cheeks and neck. It stung and numbed his cut lips. He perched the glass on his belly and wiped his stinging mouth. He took another tilt at the glass and this time he did better.

"My mouth don't work so good right now," he said and made a broken smile.

"It will."

"Now I can see you better," he said, after another slopping drink.

His brother struck a match and lit the smoky wick in a Coleman lantern for them to eat by.

"How long have I been sleeping?"

"The yesterday before the yesterday before. Maybe longer."

"I was somewhat crazy for a time."

"Some business."

"I died out there," he said.

"You look alive to me."

"The person I was died out there."

"Quit your talk like that. Eat some of this food."

"I was dead and now I am someone else," Napoleon said.

"Who?"

"I don't know who, but I am different now."

"For Christ's sake."

"Do you think there's more?" he said.

"More what?"

"Just more," he said, letting his hand to indicate expanse.

"No," his brother said, picking up his glass and looking into it.

"I don't think so either."

"It's still a good question to ask from time to time."

"Just to remind yourself."

"Yes," Xenophon said.

"Nobody gives a fuck."

"Not really."

His brother looked up from his glass. He told him how when they found him he wasn't alive, at least as they could tell. As best they could figure it, he was dead of sun.

"Where we found you," he said, holding his hand as if settling air, "we cut no trail of man nor animal, not even your trail into there. Nothing."

"Bandy?"

"Nothing."

"Bad damn luck that one."

"That one didn't know his ass from his elbow."

"He was a good one," Napoleon said, though he knew the boy was useless and at times could be pretty mouthy.

"He wasn't bad."

"Bandy was coming along so good," he persisted, and to that his brother shrugged and took a pull from his drink. Napoleon tipped out his own glass into his mouth until it was empty and held it up for another.

"Teddy," his brother called out, an invitation to eat some food and have a drink, but the Apache ignored him.

"I thought I might get in the stock tank tonight," he said. "Soak a little."

"That's a good idea."

His brother poured more drinks and then another pair after the third and they continued their drinking in the last shards of daylight.

"I'll tell you what that horse did," he said, and then he told how the Rattler horse bit the face off the man.

"He weren't no shy horse."

He paused, a hand over his forehead, and sighed deeply. Tonight he felt the loss of the Rattler as acutely as he felt the loss of the men. His brother suggested they have a drink to the Rattler horse and filled their glasses again with chipped ice and whisky.

"There ain't nothing more to say," his brother said, holding up his glass. "Some don't make it."

The whisky was the best medicine to be drinking and in memorializing the Rattler horse he remembered how a life might be and the thoughts in his mind became well built for a time and were as if printed black on a white card.

Outside the lanterns were being lit and their yellow circles of light were merging into one. Inside, the tent blued and shadowed, but as always there was enough light to drink.

From two soldiers passing by came a snip of conversation.

"Where's Dolly?"

"She's got the grippe. A temperature of one hundred and four degrees."

"Sick?"

"Sick as a bastard."

These passing conversations were as if their own and human voice sufficient enough that they did not need to talk. They watched Teddy's hands in the opening, as he worked the horsehair, the diamond-patterned macardy emerging from his side.

"What do you think it is?"

"Reins."

"Where'd he learn that? The reservation?"

"Prison, I think."

"Same difference."

It was then the chaplain came to call. The chaplain was a jolly fellow, a friend to everyone. But he thought the chaplain was a fool. He never had any use for religion anyway. He could not understand the idiocy of finding goodness in things evil and was scornful of such thinking. The man meant no more than a tick to him. Neither Teddy nor his brother were about to admit him entry, but drinking as he was, he waved them off and the bustling man made his entrance.

"What happened out there?" the chaplain said.

"Who wants to know?"

"A Baldwin-Felts agent has arrived," the chaplain said, and explained the agent was a representative of Preston's family.

"It'd take days to tell."

"Can you tell me about his final moments?"

"Who?"

"Champ Preston's."

"There ain't nothing to tell," Napoleon said.

"He was shot?"

"Among other things."

"What other things?"

"It don't matter and knowing doesn't change anything."

"He didn't say anything before he died?"

"Why?"

"They'll want to know everything."

"When they do they'll wish they hadn't."

"How can this happen?" the chaplain fretted.

"War is war," he said. "It ain't a new idea."

"It was God reminding us of his presence."

"I don't believe I needed the lesson."

"I will pray for you," the chaplain said.

"You prick. Who will pray for you?"

Later that night he eased himself over the side of the stock tank and into the night-cooled water. At first he found relief and then suddenly he desperately needed to get out. He had the overwhelming sense of being weighed down and drowned. He cried out and flailed his way back over the edge where his brother helped him drag himself over the side where he flopped down into the mud.

The capacious blisters that covered his body had filled with tank water and were dragging him down and this had caused his panic. When he struggled to his feet the blisters were ballooned in great filled sacks on his back and legs and thighs and arms. When he stood, they drained of their fluid and water and it jetted from him in a dozen spurting leaks.

The next morning his burned dead skin was yellow and crusted. His brother methodically peeled it from his body in tattered sheets. With scissors he snipped away the dead skin as close to the living skin as he dared and applied a wash of cider vinegar to his burns. He could feel the heat's rapid evaporation from his skin and suffered another bout of body shivers and teeth chattering. His brother cracked eggs over him and when the albumen dried he rolled him up in the sheeting and lay on top of him, but the shakes had lessened over the days and were not so severe. Finally they subsided. His skin relieved, he dozed.

The next night he went back into the stock tank again where he floated underneath the stars and breathed the warm night air with a dozen horses in attendance, drinking, snorting, and waffling their open nostrils on his head and neck and shoulders.

He spread his fingers and let his palms touch the water. There came the sharp yodeling bark of a coyote across the dark plain and then it was silent again. In his mind he rode out and entered another valley of sameness. He rode in on campfires and listened without being seen. At each turn there seemed to be an unfolding, a revealing, a presentation of what was simple in element and complex in nature. He'd become a creature of darkness. The pain inside him was becoming only the barb of memory to him.

"Tell me again how it went," his brother said, gratefully intruding on his thoughts.

"It went some big," he said, his mind returning to the Andalusian and the woman who rode it.

"How big?"

"It went like it had a fire inside. Like its joints were knit from spring steel."

"And the other horses?"

"Two of them were golden duns with tiger eyes. They carried the heads of kilt men."

"The others?"

"I already told you."

"Tell me again."

The next day when he awoke he was ambulatory and felt as recovered as he would ever be. He dressed himself and ate in the great kitchen while the fat cook sweated over his stoves. From the firing range he could hear the threading fire of the machine guns. The Mexican serving girls came and went, lugging out platters full of food and returning with empty ones. He was slow to realize, but then understood how every last one of them knew his story, knew what recently occurred. They said nothing to him but kept his plate full. They would have spoken to a dog but not to him.

20

L IFE IN THE ARMY was a thin empty ritual, even when wounded and healing, broken and mending, burned and growing new skin. Death was the same way. It was slow or fast or somewhere in between, except with death you did not come back and you could not use yourself again.

Word came to him they'd been out looking for the men and had no luck and were waiting on his recuperation so they could learn whatever information he might have. After the chaplain's visit, his brother had refused admittance to anyone else and nobody dared to cross him. The country had been thought not dangerous, but now they knew better. They also knew it might be dangerous tomorrow or not dangerous again and this uncertainty unsettled them. None of them had ever seen Villa. They thought they did, but they were not sure and in this way they came to be fighting no one in this land, and everyone.

The Baldwin-Felts agent, when he arrived at their tent, was a slit-eyed fellow with a lean and bitten face. He was well over six feet tall with a broad chest. He had a narrow forehead and a thin-bridged nose. He wore a well-tended handlebar mustache, sported a mallocca cane, and was dressed in tan brush drills. He carried a pencil behind his ear and had the air of one who looked down his nose at the world over the brow of that handlebar mustache.

"He needs to talk to you to ask you a few questions," his brother said, and when he shrugged—I don't care—his brother ushered him in.

"How are you doing?" the Baldwin-Felts agent asked as he extended his hand.

"I'm not feeling too chipper yet, if that's what you mean."

"You don't look too good."

"Same to you."

"I am down here to find Champ Preston," he said, and began to rub the gold knob on his cane.

"What in hell was he doing here anyways?"

"He told his mother and father he was coming here because he wanted to experience life to the very edge. What do you think of that?"

"Edge of what?"

"I don't know exactly." The Baldwin-Felts agent sighed dramatically, an enduring man who assumed responsibility for tidying the world of his benefactors.

"Who does?"

"His mother and father seem to." He took out a small notebook and the pencil from behind his ear.

"Tell them it weren't nobody's fault," he said. "Tell them he died a proper death."

"He is dead then?"

"He is dead," he said.

"You witnessed his death?"

"I seen him kilt."

The agent sighed again and took a step back. With this

declaration, by eyewitness, the agent suspended his questioning for the moment. No doubt it was the news he feared and anticipated. He bared his teeth, revealing a gold incisor.

"His remains?"

"They're dead too."

"Yes, that's what I figured. Their location?"

"Out there," he said, and cast a look southeast—still out there and he ain't coming back.

"Can you take me there?"

"I can, but you won't find nothing you'll want to find."

"His grieving family needs a body for the salve to their grief. This, of course, you understand."

"Not this body."

"Why not?"

"You'd be better off sending them a box of rocks nailed shut."

"Did he fight well?" the agent asked. "Can I at least tell them that he fought well?"

"There weren't no fight in the end."

"For instance, did he sacrifice himself so that you or others might survive the ordeal?"

"There aren't no others and there weren't no sacrifice. They did to us what they wanted to do."

"Would you say he fought like a bear cat?"

"It doesn't matter."

"Like a bear cat," he mouthed as he penciled the words into his notebook.

"Tell them he fell with his eyes facing the enemy."

"That's good. I will tell them that." He touched the pencil to the tip of his tongue and wrote down these words as well.

"After the first suffering he suffered very little and then he was dead."

"The body?"

"The body? Well, it's gone somewheres."

"Can you call to mind where exactly it happened? The more shocking the experience the more clearly one often remembers."

"There's nothing I want to remember."

To this the agent smiled. Every time he smiled he showed a mouthful of white teeth and the gold incisor beneath his mustache. He was sucking some sort of lozenge and had a habit of clicking it against his teeth. As he reviewed what he'd written, he moved the notebook back and forth before his eyes.

"What exactly are you saying?" the agent asked.

"I'm saying, he went rough."

"The body. Gentlemen, I beg you," he said, but there was no beg in his voice. "The family without the body cannot grieve. What to do about the body?" He held up his hands—cane, notebook, pencil—we have to do something.

"He needs a body," his brother said.

"Do you need his body, or will any body do?"

"I need his body," he said in final exasperation, and then told them that the General would like to see the both of them. He then removed himself from their tent and waited in the opening.

When they arrived at the General's quarters the General eyed him sternly, a look he'd seen before. The General was always admonishing him and his brother to be more careful with themselves. They were neither of them any longer the boys they had once been.

"Sit down," the General said, placing himself on the nearest chair, draping his left leg over his right.

"How are you doing?" he asked.

"As the dog says, rough."

"They say you died out there."

"I hadn't heard that."

"Well, yes," the General said. "That's what they say."

"It must be true then."

"It wouldn't be the first time."

Then the agent spoke up, reminding the General the status of the family he represented, their influence, and how grave his responsibilities. He further made it known, jabbing the brass tip of his cane into the dust, that he was empowered to honor any outstanding debts left by his man and men were already lining up with their dry and brittle papers bearing their name, the letters IOU, a number with a dollar sign, some rather substantial, and Champ Preston's signature.

Furthermore, the family would generously bear the cost of an expedition to find the body and to the man who actually found the body, there would be a substantial reward. Of these gestures he'd made the camp aware.

"Your man here is being very difficult," he said in conclusion.

"And your man was a peckerhead and a smirking bastard," the General declared.

"He was gaining experience. We'll soon need all the leaders we can muster."

"Experience for what? His was a mind not enlarged one iota by anything it experienced."

"I am sure his father will appreciate the observation. His father is a very influential man."

"I don't give a rat's ass about his father," the General said.

"The nation is going to war."

"Go to war? You think we have any business going to war? Look inside that crate you are sitting on."

The crate was draped with a tarp and used as a bench.

"Open it," the General said, flashing the back of his hand, and when the man did he found it to contain lances.

"Lances," the General said with disgust. "They send me lances."

"Nevertheless."

"Your man was a man with a reckless ass," the General told the agent, "and I put up with him, but I'd not take him into any army of mine."

"Be that as it may General, he is my man."

"Leave us alone here," the General said, and with that the agent was dismissed.

Alone, the three men did not stand on the empty ceremony of rank. The General pulled at his chin and mentioned he needed to find a razor blade somewhere. Outside, a pickup game had begun and men were throwing a football back and forth. Skirls of dust scraped by as the wind made a brief tearing sound and then it was quiet again and he could almost hear the rivings of blown sand finding a new place on the earth until blown again.

Napoleon felt the presence of his brother, standing behind him at the tent's opening, arms folded, chin on his chest, one foot in front of the other—that's how he was.

For the longest time no man broke the spell of silence. They were long past acknowledging the trials of their existence, the daily boredom, the sudden violence.

He believed the General in that moment was experiencing again the loss of his family. One of his best and most beloved men had returned from the dead, but his wife and his little girls had yet to do so. How much longer would he have to wait for them to return from the dead?

"Give me your thoughts," the General finally said.

"They had a cache of goods and stores stol'd from here."

"Who were they?"

"I have never seen the likes of them before."

"Do you know anything about a map?"

"No, sir."

"Every god damn jerk-off in this army thinks Preston held a treasure map."

"Just a bunch of fuck-offs if you ask me."

"I won't ask you to make peace with this man," the General said. "But you know as well as I do these men will not rest until they find who did this and give to them an ass-whuppin'. That means a lot of innocent people."

"I will not make peace with the man, but I will make peace with the situation."

He knew he would have to go back out so as not to deprive the men of a possible bounty. He knew if he did not go, the men would extract vengeance on every unfortunate they encountered who could not explain himself.

21

THE CAMP IN MORNING was a lowing and braying racket. They woke at four and were under way by five, the dull pallid gray of the dawn filtering its shuttered red light into the darkness. The horse he rode that morning was the Blue horse, the high-white blue-black sabino with the two blue eyes. Whereas the Rattler horse was the spirit of evil, the Blue horse was friendly and could not help but seek affection. It wished to be petted and nibbled him with its lips until he did.

His brother rode a powerful seventeen-hand chestnut, a brown-coated horse with a long mane and tail. The chestnut was a most skillful and well-knitted animal and he'd not seen a more handsome clean-built and graceful horse. With the subtlest gesture of hand the horse made right and left and stopped on a dime. It cut turns like a knife and did not so much run as it flew and danced. He smiled and wondered how long before the animal would disappoint and fall out of favor.

In the past he was often mistaken for his brother but not any longer. His face was cut and broken and changed forever and now it was only his own. And something else — it was as if the aura of the brothers was broken, the mysterious nimbus of their remote autonomy had been breached. For most men this was troubling. The brothers were so capable they made other men lazy and dependent. Other men were now emboldened: the envious and resentful, the invidious. These were the men who remembered every slight, every warning, every reprimand. These were the fatuous, the strivers, the self-opinionated. They were the mediocrity that knows nothing higher than itself and in their minds they'd been mistreated and were now the aggrieved.

This he sensed as they rode out that morning. If his brother sensed it also, he did not know. If he did he would not have cared. A man to him was less than a horse and not more than a dog or a toad. So deep were his convictions in this regard they were beyond the comprehension of all but the Apache or the horse itself, or the dog, or the toad.

They broke from the plain and were following a small alkaline streambed, dry and dusty, in the direction of a distant grove of cottonwoods. They'd left behind the train tracks, the cartage road, the abandoned hacienda when late that afternoon a dry storm broke and day lightning struck clean as a razor. Breathing on this day was as if breathing the air of a furnace and he could not help but continually shade his eyes with his hand and stare at the horizon as if he knew what was there and waiting to be seen.

All that morning they'd set a hammering pace, the horses' bodies lathered with oily sweat. Only when the sun was getting well up in the sky he swung their trail in the direction of a stone tank where they watered. They could have stopped at noon or pushed straight on through.

He let the stop be enough to rest the horses. A great wave of hot air swept by, filling their lungs with heat. The moment was so hot that to breathe deeply was to choke and cough.

"It's hot today, just plain hot,'" someone said.

"Hot? I think it's damn cold myself. I wish I had my blanket," someone answered.

Some half-wild horses came to the edge of a hill. They caught his brother's eye and he stopped. The horses stamped and snorted and stepped in their direction. He knew his brother would leave off the search and go after them if he thought even one of interest. The horses fluttered and panicked and ducked away and there being none of particular interest he let them go.

All that morning Xenophon stayed close by his side, for the most part silent unless someone needed a bawling-out.

"I am sick of wet-nursing these fucking neck riders," he said, "every one of them." Looking for the body of this man, he could not think of a more foolhardy way to spend his time.

"What time is it?" Napoleon asked him when he'd calmed down.

"Noon, I'd say. Why?"

"I'm tired."

"You'll get over it."

"No. I don't think it's the kind of tired you get over."

He was tired. He wanted a room and a goose-down bed. He wanted a square meal, a shave, a hot bath. He didn't know what all he wanted beyond that, but he knew what he didn't want and he didn't want what he had and he didn't want where he was. He wanted to think clearly again and live without the guilt he felt for losing the men: Bandy, Extra Billy, Stableforth, Turner, and even Preston.

"What made you come out here?" Napoleon asked him.

"I do not want these brainless bastards ruining any of my horses."

This is what his brother said, but he suspected another reason and one having to do with his own understanding of the men they rode with, the men in their command with prospects of bounty.

"It takes little carelessness to disable a horse," his brother said. "You care for the horse first and yourself last." He was strangely enough their greatest defender and yet capable of working them to an inch of their lives. But he asked no more of the horse than he asked of himself.

Napoleon held a palm to his forehead and stared intently at the land before the horizon where a flash of light had shown. They climbed the red sun-baked rocks of the plateau and with a pocket mirror signaled across the valley. It wasn't long before a signal came back.

"There's something there," he said.

The Blue horse crabbed sideways and he looked to where his brother was pointing and he saw it too. There was a critter walking backward dragging a half-eaten carcass. It was a feral dog or a coyote, maybe a wolf. But there was something else and it was the strangest thing he saw. It was not important, but he could not tell what it was.

It was here the Jenny found them, buzzing overhead with the intention of spotting and directing their way.

His brother turned in the saddle as the column closed, the Smith boys coming up first.

"Smith," he said.

"Yessir."

"Not you. The other Smith."

"Yessir!"

"You do not hit that horse," he bawled at the soldier, and raising an admonitory finger, he said, "That horse has a muscle cramp. You get off that horse and you walk it out."

"I miss that old Rattler horse," Napoleon said.

"That horse were as sure footed as a mule," his brother said.

"I hope we don't find it," he said, meaning the worst.

"Tell me again about the horse she rode."

"It was a beauty," he said. "About the most beautiful horse a horse can be."

"I would love to see that horse someday."

"It was a gifted horse."

"A royal horse."

"What do you think that was back there?"

"You saw it too?"

"Yes."

"Just one of those things."

"That's what I thought."

The first one they found they could smell the decay a mile away. The flensers had been at work. His naked body looked parboiled by the sun. He was hung upside down from the stark white branch of a dead cottonwood. He'd been belly cut and leg cut and his skin dragged off him so a whole other body shape sharing the one head hung down below.

On the rocks around the man were perched the vultures. They carried the scavengers featherless head and neck. They were not moving because when they looked at the men on horseback they only saw scavengers like themselves.

"Do you think he's one of ours," one of the troopers was saying.

"I wouldn't know how to tell," another said.

"He's too tall to be a greaser. How tall would you say he is?"

"I can't tell. He is upside down."

"It's still the same length, you fucknut."

"Whoever did this needs to bounce at the end of a rope."

"I just hope he was dead," the Baldwin-Felts agent said.

"If he were what would have been the point?" his brother said.

"An artist with a knife," Goudge said. "I'll give 'em that."

"This needs to be investigated," the Baldwin-Felts agent said. "They can't do that to an American."

"When are you going to get your head out of your ass?" Xenophon said as he rolled a cigarette.

"That ain't one of us. I think it's the dynamiter," Napoleon said.

"What makes you say that?"

"Just a feeling. He signed on and took their money and didn't know what he claimed to know. I'll say one thing. He didn't lack for hide."

The chaplain and the photographer drew closer. The chaplain stooped down on one knee and began to pray at the feet of the boy dynamiter. The Jenny flew over, its engine coughing.

When the chaplain stood again, he said, "Nothing is so solemn as a man's last moments of life."

"He'll just be a hole in the ground, is all," Napoleon said.

When the chaplain protested he told him to take his form of mental illness somewhere else. The photographer was already returning with the weight of his equipment on his shoulder.

"What do you want to do, sir?" one of the troopers asked him.

He nodded toward the Baldwin-Felts agent. "How about this body?" he said. "Will this one do for you?"

"Not if it isn't him."

"Cut him down and bury him," he told the dismounted troopers. The photographer asked for a moment as he erected his tripod, his camera fixed on top and the men held back so the photographer could do his work.

Miles in the distance his brother glassed a column of vultures riding what little eddies the upper air afforded. He yelled out for the men to come on and get the work done of cutting the man down. He could tell his brother's agitation as it was translated to the chestnut whose broad hooves cut patterned didoes in the dirt.

"Goudge," Napoleon yelled, "get it done. We're wasting time," and then he turned the Blue horse and was following his brother who'd broke for the vultures.

The gyring vultures guided them on and after a long time they came across another dead, a Yaqui in rictus clutching an open gunnysack at the mouth of a canyon. There was a rattlesnake fastened to his face, its fangs set deep, attached to his cheek. The outriders had already arrived and were crouched on their haunches and staring into the man's claggy, dead eyes.

"He's dead all right," one of the outriders said.

"He's jined the dead," the other one said, looking up at them. "Snake bit him."

"That'll mean fewer idiots around," the first one said.

He led them on and soon they entered into the canyon. The air by moment was burdened with the stench of death. As the rock walls rose and closed he felt again to be entering the whelm of his greatest loss and it wasn't long before they found three more and these were their men and there were horses too, the Rattler horse amongst them. He looked out at the sight before them.

Great swarms of flies occupied the air of the killing floor. They buzzed and lit and stung. Someone behind him swore softly. Then they all fell silent, taking their own hard looks.

Napoleon dismounted and stood again in the hard place where he'd fought and lost. He felt to be migrating close up under the sky, how terrible was this moment on earth when the earth split open and devils poured out.

They'd been stripped of their tunics and trousers, their boots and hats and weapons and the horses of their shoes and furnishings. They were naked and their sun-drained and waxlike bodies torn open where coyotes and vultures had been at them. Their bodies looked parboiled and then baked in the sun. They had certain characteristics that men have, but they were not like men at all. The scene was prehistoric, a windswept abattoir, silent music playing through the ravaged rib cages. After the first time you looked at them they were not hard to look at.

He kneeled down and laid his hand on the fine flat shoulder of the Rattler horse. The magnificent horse had given him all that it had to give. There was nothing more he could have asked.

"That would be Turner," Napoleon said.

"How do you know?" the agent asked.

"A double-barreled shotgun don't leave much face bone."

In some places the earth was no more than spilled powder and in other places the sand was hard and the black of lacquer.

He went on to identify Stableforth, the back of his skull blown away and Extra Billy, whose head was broke open. Someone had taken the time to knock out his brains after he was killed the second time.

Life had been separated from matter and all that was left now lay before him exposed and lifeless. He knew too much and he'd seen too much. It was enough. He took out a paper and his tobacco and with steady hands he rolled a cigarette.

"Look up there," someone said, and they all turned to look and to see another festooned with vultures. He hung from the rock wall, high up, his legs and arms spread wide and his chest pushed out with the contour of the rock. They could make out the bony haunches and the stringy arms. His eyes were dry holes in his head and the rock beneath his bare feet was a long ragged stain of black. It was Bandy, who tried to climb away like he was told.

That boy, he thought, was ignorant as an egg.

Men began shooting the vultures, errantly introducing enough lead into the boy's body to make it dance on its bindings.

Wheeler, his rage barely in check, flew at them until they stopped and then it was Wheeler who climbed the wall and lowered down the ragged and tattered and newly shot being that was his friend. He would not let anyone help him in this work. He cradled him gently in his arms and insisted in wrapping him in an oilcloth to take him back for a proper burial.

Napoleon watched Wheeler in his work. He flashed on a future when there would be a world of such figures. They would be found upon rocks such as this one or lying in the mud or forest or desert. They'd be floating to the bottom of the ocean. They'd be boys and women and children. They'd be young men. But who would be left to find them? The old men, that's who. The old men will endure.

Bandy, Extra Billy—they were good men, he thought. Beyond the frailties of moment and personality they were men who would fight to the last measure and what more could you ask of a man? They had no illusions of invincibility. They insisted upon no right to innocence.

"They were good men," Napoleon finally said aloud.

"They were," his brother said, and mounted the chestnut and turned the horse in the direction from which they'd come.

"This is where it ends," he said.

"Do you not remember anything more?" the agent said.

"We were on a trail and we got off the trail somewhere."

"Do you not remember where?"

"If I could remember, I wouldn't do it on your account," he said, his patience with this man now exhausted.

"I don't like it," the Baldwin-Felts agent said.

"What do you like?" Napoleon said.

The Blue horse was behind him, thrusting its nose, smooth

as silk, under his elbow. He turned to it and rubbed its fore-head. The horse lowered its head until it was pressed against his chest and he stroked its glossy neck.

"Leave it alone," Goudge said to the Baldwin-Felts agent.

"Leave it alone? How can he not remember?" The agent persisted.

When the detective would not relent his brother turned the chestnut horse fiercely and spurred forward. He rode hard the short distance he'd traveled, pulled up, and came off the animal in one motion.

It was not his brother's way to reason, or argue. His brother struck the agent and struck hard as if the man was just an-other animal wandering the earth and then he walked away to where the chestnut stood patient and quiet.

The agent lay stunned on the ground nursing the side of his head already glowing with the red bruise that would turn blue and then purple. Goudge went to him and helped him onto his feet. He sputtered with outrage and threat.

"He tried to kill me."

"You ain't dead, are you?" Goudge said.

"No."

"Then he didn't try."

"They don't turn the other cheek, mister," the first Smith said.

"They ain't even got an other cheek," the second Smith said.

He knew they'd never find Preston's body and it was point-less to try. His body would be dragged for miles, dragged un-til there was nothing left at the end of the rope. Who knew that his body wasn't still being dragged and what little of it remained was just now wearing out and dropping away and disappearing forever.

Did they really want the truth, especially this truth? Perhaps it is so; people cannot bear the mystery of disappearance. But Preston's disappearance, however unbearable, was better than the truth.

Blowing their way was a dirty smoke and soon they could hear its crackling on the air. From over sky distance came the sound of a grinding engine. The engine coughed and sputtered and went out. To the north the photographer had caught fire to the brush and to the south the Jenny had gone down beyond the sun-tinted mountains.

There was a mottling of western light. The deaths of the men was an episode closed, their remains wrapped and trussed in a tight bundles, their bodies as light and fleshless as kindling. When the moon rose that night, the stars in the sky were red as blood and they were a long straggling troop returning from their mission. The pilot of the Jenny, his leg in a splint rode with them. Some men watched the stars in their coming while others sat on their horses asleep, their shoulders folded and heads bobbing. It was late that day, long past darkness, when they sifted past the fixed sentinels and back into camp. The arc lights crackled on the perimeter and then they went out.

22

MOST PEOPLE WANTED to be someone or something else but not him, not his brother. They never thought they were anything but what they were. They were cavalrymen and life on horseback was the only life they knew, and yet on this night he went to see the General, to tell him he was leaving.

"Home?" the General said.

"I'd like to see my father," he told the General.

"What about your brother?"

"Just me."

The General lifted his glasses and settled them lower on his nose that he might look over the tops of them. The two brothers were his intractable men. They were his worst soldiers but his most loyal, most dependable, most efficient, most lethal men. He could not have stood a hundred men like them because that was not how armies were made, but two, or five, that did nicely.

The General took up a piece of paper and an ink pen and asked him when he signed on, how many years ago, but he could not remember.

"A long time ago," the General said, and began writing.

It was last year the General lost his family: his wife and his little girls. They burned to death at the Presidio while he was stationed at Fort Sam Houston in San Antonio. It was in January Villa killed American mine engineers on the Chihuahua train and then two months later he'd attacked Columbus, New Mexico.

The General put down his pen and leaned over to blow the last ink dry. He took off his rimless spectacles and let them dangle at the ends of his fingers. He watched the General moving his lips as he read the orders he'd written. He put his finger on the line he was reading to hold his place before looking up. His eyes became very bright and shined in his head as if he'd seen the unseen.

"They say," he began, "that young people think they can't die. They do not understand its potential. I disagree. It is simply the fact that young people are stupid and thank you for that because we need them to fight our wars."

"Some come back alive and some don't."

"I was wondering if, when you are in that place, you know anything."

"Which place would that be?" Napoleon said.

"Heaven. Hell. Does it make much difference?"

"No. I don't believe it does."

"Either way I guess they know now." The General set down the letter and took out a cigarette and struck a match. He had a habit of lighting a match and holding it while he talked and forgetting to use it and then lighting another.

"Is this for good?" he asked, seeming to come from a trance.

"I hadn't thought about it."

"Have you ever thought about getting out altogether?"

"I can't say that I ever have."

"We've had some times," the General said.

"We have."

"I would be honored if you would have a drink with me."

The General took a bottle from a locker and two glasses and for a time they were just two old men, raw boned and hollow bellied, in the company of each other.

"I should like to meet your father some day," the General said, holding up his glass.

"My father?"

"Yes."

"He surely had himself some times."

"Tough old birds back then."

"They took a lot of killing."

"This god damn goose chase is a discredit to war."

"I hear that."

"Will you be back?" the General asked him again.

"I have not thought about it," he said, and then he said, "I suppose it depends on what I find."

"Do you think there's a lot left to find?" the General said.

"I would say we've already found plenty," he said, and the General agreed.

They finished their drinks and stepped outside into the night. Parked beside the General's quarters was an automobile, a Dodge five-passenger touring car.

"Have you thought about how you are going?" the General asked.

"I thought to hitch a ride on a truck."

"Take this car," the General said, and he agreed to do so and thanked him.

"Do you know how to drive it?"

"No."

"Do you want a driver?"

"No. I'll figure it out," Napoleon said.

The two men drew near together, and each leaned in to grasp the other's hand. They held the handshake and then they stepped back, and his orders secure in the breast pocket of his tunic, he turned and walked away.

As he made his way back to his tent he made one last pass through town. In the window of a shop the photographer rented were newly printed postcards on display. The photographer must've worked all night to have the silvery images of the dead first ready. In the air were cooking smells and the smell of the latrines and coal oil and when the air changed it was tainted with a burning smell.

At the corner to an alley he heard a faint whistle in the darkness, someone calling to him. He cocked his head and held it there without moving as he sorted out what drew his attention. He turned his head and more distinctly he heard the whistle again. He followed the sound, a young boy, down a dark weedy path that wove between buildings.

He stopped and listened to the blunt tap of a cobbler's hammer. He watched a woman washing clothes beneath the laddering light of the moon. There was the sound of a foot-powered wood lathe. The boy whistled again and he knew how he knew the boy. It was the boy who shined his boots.

He followed him down the path where he met with the smell of raw sewage and creosote, the stink of human sweat, cold blood, and caked fat. They passed a pair of gaunt and scraggly dogs that were tearing at a wet gunnysack trying to get at what was inside. Another dog slanched into his path on the way to the wet gunnysack. There was a woman milking a goat, its head was turned and its face was in her neck. The woman's eyes were like wet silver in the darkness and he realized she was blind.

The boy paused at a cross path and waited and when he caught up the boy moved on, more quickly and deeper into the labyrinth of walls and fences and garden plots. In the light of the open door he could see a woman nursing an infant. He did not know why, but the woman's look was intent and she was staring at him. She seemed to know him and this knowledge unsettled him. Sitting beside her was an old woman gone in the teeth dandling a baby. The old woman was quick eyed and threw him a nod in the direction he was going and then looked away.

They traced a long adobe wall and finally came to tall doors set in the long wall where the boy stopped and indicated he should wait before he pulled mightily at a black iron ring and disappeared though the slender swing of an opening.

Inside the door was a zaguan, a roofed passage connecting the perimeter buildings, and beyond a moonlit yard laid with cobblestones. There were bundles of hay and straw and sacks of animal feed. There was a wagon and beside it a carriage under repair, the rear axle propped on wooden barrels. Somewhere in the darkness, beneath a branchless tree, a bird fluttered in a cage. He could see a candle in a glass faintly burning in the window opening. Then it moved and disappeared and then it appeared again and it was coming in his direction.

He watched from the door shadow as the fragile light came his way across the yard, low to the cobbled ground. Behind his back, sheet lightning illuminated the earth. It was a young woman wearing a veil and she moved with the dreamy motion of drunkenness, sheltering the candle glass with her cupped hand as she wove her steps across the cobbles. The closer she came the younger she became until she was not a woman but a girl whose black hair veiled her face.

When she came abreast of him she looked up at him. She smelled of perfume. Her lips were painted carmine and her complexion pale and whited. Her other hand at the base of her throat, she held up the candle glass that he should recognize her face. In the light he could see her red lips and soft cat eyes, but the light was too thin and he did not recognize her.

She stared at him with a steady gaze and then slowly she reached back and lifted her hair from the nape of her neck.

Then he remembered her. Her screams that night in the cantina. When he heard her cry out he stood so abruptly he overturned his chair and the table and crossed the room and tore back the curtain. There was a short hallway revealed with three curtained cribs on each side. At the end of the hallway he tore back another curtain and there was Preston. He was standing in the corner, naked from the waist down and he was bleeding from the wrist where he'd been cut with a straight razor. He was hysterical, mute and trembling, for what had happened to him. On his face he wore the unnatural smile of the drunk and terrified. He stared at his wrist as if an evil newly attached.

Napoleon remembered her cowering in a corner of the room holding a hand to the side of her head and blood was seeping from between her fingers. She held her other hand to her nose where another source of blood was wetting her hand to the wrist. Her face was bruised and contorted with pain. One eye had closed. He found a white cloth and took her hand away. The round of her ear was missing. It'd been cut away from her head. He held the cloth to her wound and then covered it with her hand and pulled her head against his chest, her hand in between and he held her in his arms.

He could now see the maiming Preston had committed to her. Her cheek on that side and her forehead were still flush with traumatic bruising and this she'd tried to hide with cornstarch. Her face was still bruised and her half ear was rimed black and still crusted with a blood bandage.

She blew out the candle and reached into a pocket sewn to her skirt and removed a package wrapped in butcher paper and tied with string. She handed it to him, but when he went to open it she stayed his hand and shook her head no, he should not unwrap it, not now, and indicated, Take it away. Take it from me.

He went to speak, but she shook her head no. She closed her eyes and pressed a hand against the side of her head. She would not talk to him. There was nothing to say.

He let the package into his trouser pocket as she disappeared behind the massive wooden door and it slowly closed. From there he made his way back through the matrix of paths and alleys to the main street.

It was in front of a cantina he encountered Wheeler. A number of soldiers were lounging and smoking in the shadowy darkness. Wheeler stood in yellow light in the open doorway eating a sausage off the end of a skewer and drinking from a bottle of beer. Sitting against the wall were men perched on the hind legs of their chairs. They were half drunk, smoking, chewing, spitting, digesting. They'd brought out a watermelon and some were eating fat slices and spitting seeds into the dust. It was another night in the army for them, just like any other. They could see him coming and yet there was no sign of respect for his rank.

"Hey there, old-timer," Wheeler said.

He could taste his blood in his throat. Let it go, his mind repeated. Keep walking, he told himself, but he did not. He thought about the girl. He thought about the grief inside him.

He began walking in Wheeler's direction and Wheeler waited for him as he came on. He could not tell how much the man had been drinking. It did not seem he was drunk, but he trusted that to be the source of his insolence.

"How are you this evening?" Wheeler inquired.

"Fair. And yourself?"

"Been better. Been worse."

Wheeler bit off the last of the sausage and threw the skewer aside. The men at the wall kept sucking at the fleshy melon. Swaggering, half-drunken soldiers strolling the streets were stopping to see what was going on. Standing about, sitting in the half shadows were, no doubt, some of the very men they were hunting.

"Tell me something," Wheeler said. "Every man I ever knew was scared of getting old and dying. Is that true?"

"Dying's true," he said. He would not fall back on his rank to deal with this man. He had never done so and was not about to start.

"This country can kill you," Wheeler said.

"What country won't?" he said, squaring his shoulders to the man.

"I wouldn't know that. I haven't been everywheres else like you have." Wheeler took on a jolly face and a confident smile.

"Don't make him mad, sir. He can be mean as a cut snake." One of the other men had decided to be a part of what was happening.

"I ain't afraid of you or your brother," Wheeler said.

"No, I don't suppose you are," he said. "But I sense the fear."

"What have I got to be afraid of?"

He knew he could not make up for what happened in the desert, but he was in the mood to kill this man if he had to and he was cold to the business of it.

"You want to shed your blood?" he asked Wheeler. "You try me and I will kill you for the love of killing you."

Wheeler's mouth was finally stopped. He toed the gravel with his boot.

"Look at me when I speak to you," he said.

Napoleon looked in his eyes and willed that he should make the move to challenge him. There was nothing this fight would wash away. This was nature's work and the malice he felt was not for this man but was from the time before ancient came.

"You couldn't fight before," Wheeler said. "What makes you think you can now?"

Napoleon took one step and swung as hard as he could from the muscle ridged across his shoulders. It was a vicious punch and under his knuckles he could feel the crush of Wheeler's nose. The man went down on his knees his hands at his face and the red blood blossoming beneath them. He let the man bleed and then he swung again, another vicious blow and felt the man's jawbone breaking from its hinge and giving way and the man was lying in the street, his broken face torn with agony.

Inside his guts he was dry as horn and was as if he willed the instant of pain the man experienced. He wanted it to be something alive that would never die and the man would feel it forever, even after his death.

Then his blood quieted. He stood over the fallen man in watery moonlight and looked into the shadows of the porch. He took out a bought cigarette and struck a match. Wheeler made a choking sound and then he was hacking up blood from his throat and spitting out the blood. He opened his hand and looked at his teeth and then covered his bloody face again.

Under the shadow of the cantina roof were the sons of bitches of human nature. Look at me, he thought. Take a look. The world's full of no-good people, he thought, and he included himself. Nothing made sense to him except what was primitive and vengeful.

"Put your ear here and listen," he said, leaning down to where Wheeler lay paralyzed by his pain.

The man moaned and gurgled for the blood in his throat, from the breakage his face and jaw had sustained. His eyes were pinched shut from the rack of pain that his face had become, but he gestured. He waved a hand in the air, as if he was reaching for something he could not see.

"You remember me," he said to Wheeler. "Don't you ever forget me."

Then he walked away and the men came onto the dusty street, into the moonlight to watch him go, complete in their arrogance and their stupidity and their renewed respect for him.

He chastised himself for losing his temper but not very much. He knew he could not reason with this man and that men like him had to be shamed and that's what he did. He knew he had abased himself in confronting the man the way he did, but he also knew he had no other choice if he was ever to return.

He touched at the package he carried in his pocket. There was little point in opening it. He already knew what was inside.

23

WHITE GULLS SCULLED the air the morning of his leaving. He packed coffee, corned beef, two bread, sugar, condensed milk, gasoline. He carried in his breast pocket a pair of blue-tinted sunglasses.

The chaplain had placed a Bible on the backseat. He savored the thought of throwing it out the window.

Early that first day he'd passed through a long caravan of mule wagons loaded with baled hay and bales of straw and then he was alone on the long dusty road and then coming against him was a continuous stream of supplies and men.

There was no heater in the car, but he had a blanket and a quart of whisky and after a swig he'd bite off a chaw from a plug of tobacco he carried and this kept him awake. He continued on by starlight so determined to leave the godforsaken country of recent events. His thoughts in these hours, a constant threat to his sanity, he controlled, but admitted he'd been scared of dying and he'd never been scared in his life. Then he told himself: It weren't nothing to me. And repeated: It weren't nothing.

He crossed the international line at Columbus, where massed was a vast depot of men and horses, artillery and armored vehicles and he pushed on from there.

The roads were local affairs connecting one town to the next, or the road was the wide beaten path that paralleled train tracks. By now he'd come to like sitting in the soft front seat and watching the road slide by. Remarkable to him was the number of people who'd poured into the country since the last time he traveled it. They raised grain crops, herefords, and shorthorns. They'd built houses, barns, and silos. They were a busy and striving people making something where there was nothing and the nothing was disappearing.

One night he slept in a cemetery, having jounced through the swung-open wrought-iron gates in the pitch of night and thinking he found a park of sorts or the estate of a great man. Another night he parked the automobile in an open field on the edge of a town. When he awoke men and boys were gathering in the field to play baseball. They were staring into the automobile at him sleeping as if he'd arrived from the coming time.

When he awoke they told him he was in Texas and this he did not know. They asked him to call balls and strikes and later the women came with lemonade, fried chicken, and hot dumplings made of cabbage and pork and they ate beneath a shading pavilion. He determined them a community of Germans of an old religion. The men wore boiled white shirts, black trousers with black suspenders and broad brimmed black felt hats. The boys dressed similarly and the women and girls were equally plain in the cotton dresses they wore. They were pleasant company. After the first questions they were content to not ask anymore and seemed grateful for his presence.

He came into the grass country: grama, curly mesquite,

bluestem waist high. There was an abundance of quail and prairie chickens, sawing grasshoppers, indolent and treacherous hornets, and on occasion he spotted an antelope.

The light over the prairie was thick and opaque with carried liquid. Dry lightning silently forked in the blue covering darkness. The prairie was being uprooted and turned into a sea of wheat and one night he watched the horizon burn blood red, a wheeling fire on the prairie, and then it disappeared.

There were moments when he had the feeling there was another beside him. Another who walked with him and rode with him and sat with him in the automobile, an invisible who held a visible presence in his mind. There were moments when he was sure he saw this other, but on this night there were no ghosts of dead men, no shadowy presences, no fears, no haunts.

Overhead was the quiet gathering and dispersing of clouds. There was the star-bright sky, so clear this night, he could see stars behind stars. He wondered on the dead eyes of his fallen men. He could not shake the proximity of recent blunt death. It was as close as his mind. He waved at the air in front of his face, a gesture he habited to shoo away such thoughts.

Sometimes the road bore off in a direction that was not his and other places the road petered out, but rather than turn around and retrace himself he drove overland on the hardened prairie, north by northeast, until he picked up another road that suited the direction of his intention.

Soon it would be autumn. He thought autumn light old light and come from far away. It was light that was bright and sorrowful and dense and galvanic. It lacquered the world with its brilliance and increased by day, and when the sun set down it left you tired, cold and wanting. He would be home by then. He'd sit on the porch and feel himself not moving.

As he rolled along he wondered who lived and who was dead. Would he find an old rocking man and a fallen-in cabin? He questioned his father's ability to die. He doubted him capable of dying, and if he wasn't, this would be his only incapacity.

Slowly, but surely, time was curing his memory.

He started again before daylight, leaving Oklahoma and crossing into Kansas. The road was hard packed and white in the sun. At first he was not tired, but after a few hours he was more tired than if he'd been driving all day. The road was deeply rutted and so the going was very slow. All that day a hot wind blew across his face and stole his breath and dried his mouth. It was no cloying wind that teased and sickened the stomach but a strong hot wind that lifted the dust, scored the earth, and emptied the lungs. But now there was no wind.

He stopped and walked away from the automobile and onto the land to piss. The absence of sound, of the thrumming engine, was overwhelming. He carried on his person the .45, his tobacco, a spoon. To stand without moving made him weak. His business finished, he walked on, his stiff boots, meant for riding and not walking, galled his feet. As he walked he raised clouds of grasshoppers clacking and sizzling in the air about his trouser legs.

He lit his cigarette, naturally cupping the match to hide the flame, and then smoked it, shielding the ember. These days on the road, cooking over an open fire had been the most peaceful he'd experienced. Then a loneliness like a mist came over him. He felt it in his arms and legs, a vulnerability in his chest. He was alone out here and unmoored on this vast sea of grassland. He missed his brother.

Black storm clouds were massing in the north the whole of that day and the sky was hardened. He could not remember the last time he was rained on. Let the weather be foul. It didn't matter to him. He returned to the automobile, let out the clutch, and rammed the car along a stretch of black deeply rutted soil. He drove on until he dozed at the wheel and then he pulled off and let his head go back against the seat. Inside, he was wearied on the verge of collapse. He righted himself and continued on.

The storm moved east, and a sozzling rain was still falling when he entered the wet band the storm left behind. The wheels of the Dodge slithered in the mud, and then there was a lull in the rain and the day turned hot and steamy. The deep ruts were left awash and they captured the wheels and guided the automobile. The automobile ruddered in the throws of the wet channels and began to cough and sputter and lose power. He pushed on, the steering wheel snapping right and left and the one time he let it go so as to not break a wrist.

Then the automobile spun and the engine wound and then stopped as if held by a sudden hand. The wheels were stogged deep in clayey mud. He'd bogged himself down right to the axle and would need a team of horses to haul out.

Over the next rise he hailed a wheat farmer working a field and found out a town was not so far. There was an auto mechanic there in case he needed one and so arranged for the farmer to tow the automobile out of the bog when his day was done. He himself would continue on afoot.

Before long the road turned smoldering hot. He came to men in striped trousers, their bodies stripped to the waist. They were chained at the ankles and in cadence shuffled forward and let down their slingblades to cut back the grassy ditches. Two men stood quietly harnessed to a scoop shovel being loaded. They were guarded by men on horseback, Winchesters perched upright on their thighs. He'd one time known a trooper from Mississippi, a former trustee who'd been pardoned for shooting a runner. He remembered him a crack shot on horseback.

He decided he'd wait for the wheat farmer. He turned around and went back to the stogged automobile, the water already cooked from the ruts.

That evening the western sky was heart red. The farmer broke him out and directed him to a place where a thin stream ran through the land and told him he could camp there for the night. He pulled off the road and bumped onto the field. He drove the Dodge across where had stood the heavy crops of grain. He came off the dry flat land and entered a band of cottonwoods that densified until there were only trees and he was passing through chains of last light and shadow and arrived at a barbed-wire fence and a place where the creek pooled flat and brown. Hung on the fence was a killed snake belly side up. An appeal for rain recently answered.

Down by the creek he found a stone fire ring and an iron grate hanging from a tree. There were steel rods to make a spit and kindling and firewood beneath a ragged tarp. At the creek bank he discovered arrowheads that'd been washed to the light. Flash floods were as dangerous as prairie fires and twisters. Still, he wanted to be near the pooling water and kicked up dry cow manure for his fire.

After so many months in the desert the grasses and flowers were an experience for him. Like a sleepwalker, he continued on. His boots wetted with the rising dew as he crossed the field. Even in this dry land, the air was dense with moisture and filled his lungs to capacity.

He sprawled in the silky grass beneath the spangle of stars. He gathered bunches in his fingers. The grass gave off no scent, but pulled from the earth came a sweetness. He found the far bright star. These small things, he thought, and for a time the tight band was wrested from across his chest and the sound of the purling creek entered his mind.

He wished for more rain. He wished for it to come down from the sky and wash across his face. He returned to the fire ring and started a fire and laid the grate across the heating stones. He fed the fire and sulfur teals of flame swam like water beneath the iron skillet when he set it on the grate. The skim of grease was heating and when it began to pop he'd fry his potatoes and when they were done he'd scrape them to one side and crack his eggs.

24

H E'D FINISHED OFF his eggs and potatoes and was spit roasting a chicken when he heard a human sound. Beyond the glow of the small fire the night was blued and the grasses tipped in silver. Someone was approaching in the darkness, their trousers making a wisping sound as they waded through the grass. He touched at the .45 he carried in the shoulder rig.

"Halloo," came a long call from the darkness. It was the wheat farmer coming through the moon's light.

"Come on in," he said.

"I called out because I didn't want to get shot," the farmer said with humor. He wore a blue short-sleeved shirt, blue overalls, and a blue bandanna loosely knotted at his neck. He carried a walking stick he swept before him.

"Probably not a bad idea," he said.

"She sent me to bring you this pie."

"Please thank her for me," he said, accepting the pie tin into his hands.

"Why yes, of course," the farmer said, becoming at ease and then he said, "Is that a government automobile?"

"Yes, it is."

"Where are you driving it to?"

"Driving east."

"You look about used up," the farmer said.

"I been eatin' dry bread, if you know what I mean."

"Where you coming from?'

"Down Mexico."

"You don't say. What's it like down there?" He spoke as if Mexico were an invisible star.

"All's that land does is hold the earth together."

From the darkness came the spearing cry of a prey bird. The farmer noted the cry for how unlucky the creature and adjusted his seat closer to the fire where he poked at it with his walking stick.

It was strange to sit with this man. That this man should have a life, that he should have a family and his mouth would move, his hands gesture. At first he wasn't sure of the man because he did not know him, but he was harmless enough.

"It's a fine night," the farmer said.

"Yes, it is," he said, looking up and finding the star of his destination.

"I just wish it wasn't so dark."

"What is it you want to see?" he asked, but the farmer didn't say anything. He walked his stick about the edge of fire.

Then he said, "Which rumor do you believe? That Villa was paid to attack Columbus by the Germans?"

"I don't have anything to tell about that."

"How about the war overseas? Are we going to get in?"

"You'll have to ask the War Department," Napoleon said.

"I thought you might know and that's why you are here."

"Why am I here?"

"To set up a recruitment. To get ready. She thought that."

"Who?"

"My wife. We've got two boys. One of them is old enough."

"I don't know anything about it."

"How long have you been on the road?"

"Not long long."

"There's a town that way," the farmer said, and pointed with his stick, its embered tip aiming the way.

It was easy to tell there was something on the farmer's mind. The farmer told him not to wait on his account and to go ahead eat his chicken. Then he spoke again.

"She apologizes. We have the two sons and she doesn't want them getting any ideas."

"I understand."

"When do you think we'll get in?"

"Hard to say," Napoleon said.

"I wish I could see the point of it, but I cannot," the farmer said. Then he told how the war overseas had been very good to him, what with wheat a dollar and seventy-five cents a bushel. His face was no longer an exhausted face, but just the tired face of a man after a long day's work that was ended until tomorrow.

"Tomorrow will be better than today," the farmer sighed.

"We believe that, don't we. The future will be better than the past."

"Yes, I think we do."

"Why do we believe it?" Napoleon wondered aloud.

"I don't exactly know," the farmer said.

"I don't either," he said, and tossed more of the dried cow manure into the fire.

"They say the rain follows the plow, but I don't believe it. As good as it looks, it doesn't look good."

"Kind of late for not believing," he said, and with his knife he pried a leg from the chicken. Fat sizzled into the fire. He offered it to the farmer who took it and then he pried away the other leg for himself.

"In this land these people are all good republicans," the farmer said.

"I suppose they are."

"I wouldn't live in any other land."

He finished off the leg he was eating and the farmer finished his and they threw the bones in the fire. The farmer smacked his lips and thanked him. He then drew a pipe and packed the bowl with tobacco he carried in a leather pouch. The pouch was strung to a brass safety pin fastened at the breast pocket of his blue cotton shirt. He struck a match off the seat of his pants.

"There was a killing recently," the farmer said, reaching out with the match that he might light his cigarette. "It has people on edge."

"Who was kilt?"

"Two little girls," the farmer said, and told how a week ago two white sisters ages sixteen and twelve had gone together to pick berries three miles north from town. The family dog returned home alone.

"You have killed men?" the farmer asked.

"I have killed men," he said.

"In war."

"In the trade of war."

"Does that weigh on your mind?"

"My conscience?"

"Your conscience."

"No," Napoleon said.

"Mexico?"

"Mexico, yes."

"According to the physician's report, the girls had been out-raged, meaning raped."

"I know what it means," Napoleon said.

"They caught the fella did it. They lynched him from the bridge crossing."

"Is that how they do people around here?"

"I believe so. Is it different where you come from?"

"No. Not much I suppose."

"People around here don't wonder what their lives are to be. If they do, they don't share their thoughts with anyone."

"You think they got the right man?"

To this question the farmer shrugged and it was clear to see his mind attach to a memory he felt as sharp as thorns.

From his pocket he took out the package given him by the girl in Mexico. He held the package in his lap and with his folding knife he slit the string that tied the package. He carefully unfolded the paper, wrap by wrap. It was a swedge-tipped knife with deeply cut finger choils. It had a white jigged-bone handle and nickel silver bolsters and was stained with blackness.

"What'cha got there?" the farmer asked.

"Nothing," he said. "Just a knife."

"We lost a little girl a while back," the farmer said. "They say if you wear out two pairs of shoes in this country you never leave. They didn't say anything about losing children."

"I am sorry for your loss," he said, and thought how there was history in all men's lives. He had his own and this was this man's, the loss of the little girl child. He pinched the ember from his cigarette and booted it out. Then he stripped the tobacco from the stub back into his pouch.

"It's good pie," the farmer said. "She makes a good pie."

"I look forward to it."

"Do you have anyone? A wife or the like?"

"No. Nothing like that."

"When are you coming back this way?"

"I don't know that I ever will."

"Well, when you do I'll still be here."

"Give these to your boys," he said, and handed over the arrowheads he fished from his pocket.

"They're all gone now. The buffalo and the Indians."

"I was around here when they wasn't." He pinched off a nostril and blew his nose into the dirt. Then he pinched off the other one and did it again.

"It was a long long time ago."

25

THAT NIGHT WHEN he unrolled his blanket in the grass he had the odd thought he was too tired to sleep. He imagined a pillow, stuffed with goose down, where he could rest his head and settled back and let his head to the good soft pillow he imagined.

This land had surely taken some years off his life and he could not blame the landed men on a night such as this, their cool rooms and their beds so soft. Their houses ticking quietly as they shrugged off the day, as they ever so slowly responded to the earth's invisible movement.

He rubbed at his bloodshot eyes. He could not remember the last bed he'd slept in, but that was okay. The bed he'd made for himself was comfortable enough. No matter how tired he was from the road and how comfortable his made bed, for a long time his mind wandered at the edge of wakefulness.

The night heavied and he wondered if there would be a storm again. He reached out, his waterproof close by, the knife with the jigged-bone handle, the .45 closer.

The dead began to unbury themselves.

Let it happen, he thought.

He wondered how many more days to the river and the St. Louis Bridge. Soon there'd come a night, the automobile running smoothly beneath a moon set in the sky like a silver dollar, the western side of the big river, running north atop a levee, the pale-faced moon bloody on the red earth where it went down to the water and the moon path whitening and glittering across the water, the stars so deep in the water and their lights beneath the water's surface and a shooting star coming out of the sky and lasting but a few bright seconds before disappearing, the river's glister shining and the braiding channels lit from within by the path of submerged and burning light.

He can see the river. He can see its surface catching a dim blur of lights. In his eye he catches the bounce of glitter-white light coming off the wide flowing water. Then there is a bending in the river and it is gone. Then the bridge and across the river. It will be soon now when the automobile will rattle over the high bridge above the wide water and cross to the other side.

He smiles and in the forward cast of his mind he can see all the way home to a day in the future when they'll come for him.

They'll be sitting on horseback outside the door, his brother and Teddy, and between them the Rattler horse on lead. When the Rattler horse sees him, a black sideways gleam comes into its eye. The horse nickers and stamps and the jar of its hooves cracks the frozen ground beneath. Sparks flash from steel shoes against rock and ice. He touches at the Rattler horse and under his touch he feels its trembling neck. He drags his fingers over the hard scars where the bullets found their entry.

"That horse went for quite a wander," he says.

"It has seen more of the world than most," his brother says.

Then another rider is arriving in the dooryard and he cups a hand to shade his vision.

"There's someone wants to see you," his brother says.

The rider is bundled against the cold and invisible until he unwraps his woolen scarf and it's Bandy.

"Cold enough for you?" he says to the boy.

"Cold as the nose on a froze dog," the boy says.

That night the cold sky is smokelike and the moon orange and holds place in the sky as if set aloft from the earth solely for their benefit.

There is a flowery smell in the air, like that of a woman, strange and sourceless, and from the stables the occasional tromp of slow bodies shifting hooves. There is the murmur of a storm, currents of warm air. The stars, they pale.

Then the sky overclouds and a wind springs up and they listen to the heaving of the wind through the trees. It's a warm wind, the first warm wind in months. Ruminant and lost, the years disappear and there is a childlike look in their eyes as each man appreciates the other's silent recall.

"You find enough of what you're looking for?" his brother says.

"No. Not yet."

"Maybe you have to look harder."

"Maybe."

His brother tells him they are requested to proceed to France at as early a date as practicable.

"The General said it wouldn't be quitting if you decided not to go."

"What are you going to do?"

"Go," Xenophon said.

"I'll go then, if that's what we are doing."

"Which horse will you take?"

"I don't know. Part of me wants to leave the old cutthroat here, but I am afraid he will kill someone. What do you think?"

"Better take him. Where we're going we'll need all the killing we can get."

When they awake the winter morning is cold and purple hued. The fires are banked and the cookstove cherries at the joints.

"What o'clock is it?"

"It's six. It will take seven days to cross the ocean," his brother says, looking at his pocket watch as if it were a watch of days and not minutes and hours.

"The horses are packed?"

"Yes."

"Then perhaps we should go."

"Yes."

He steps out into the morning beneath the gray sheet of the cast sky. He takes the Rattler's face in his hands. He adjusts the headstall and tugs at the buckle on the throat latch. He draws the cinch tight and taking the reins in hand he swings up into the saddle.

The black horse his brother rides suddenly erupts in a high ballotade and then makes to the side, cantering backward on three legs. It performs a reverse pirouette with feet crossed and then moves forward with grace and tranquillity. His brother raises his hand in tierce as high as his right ear and thrusts to the front. Their father raises his own hand and they hold rigid and smiles break across their faces. The dogs—they begin to bark.

His father turns to him and salutes and he snaps off the samelike gesture and they smile on each other.

"Take keer of yourselfs," their father says.

"We will, Daddy. We will take care of ourselfs."

He knows this day is coming and when it does he will stand in something like sunlight and together they will ride out of there. It will take them fourteen days to Norfolk and seven more days to cross the ocean where they'll arrive in the green of the new spring in France.